ULYSSES
IN
SAN JUAN

BOOK 3 OF THE PUERTO RICO TRILOGY

ROBERT FRIEDMAN

BROWN POSEY PRESS

an imprint of Sunbury Press, Inc.
Mechanicsburg, PA USA

an imprint of Sunbury Press, Inc.
Mechanicsburg, PA USA

For information about special discounts for bulk purchases, please contact Sunbury Press Orders Dept. at (855) 338-8359 or orders@sunburypress.com.

To request one of our authors for speaking engagements or book signings, please contact Sunbury Press Publicity Dept. at publicity@sunburypress.com.

ISBN: 978-1-62006-044-5 (Trade paperback)

Library of Congress Control Number: 2019937718

FIRST BROWN POSEY PRESS EDITION: March 2019

Product of the United States of America
0 1 1 2 3 5 8 13 21 34 55

Set in Bookman Old Style
Designed by Crystal Devine
Cover by Terry Kennedy
Edited by Lawrence Knorr

Continue the Enlightenment!

One night after I was coming home from a walk, I wasn't sleeping so good, someone was waiting by the front of my apartment house. The guy wasn't there to greet me. He was there to mug me.

He jumped in front of me, a knife shining in his hands, an out-of-focus look shining in his eyes. He put the point of the blade by my throat and told me to give him all my money. I think I had fifty cents in change on me. My wallet was upstairs. I was about to give him my watch when I recognized him.

"Billy Greene?"

He was the young fellow who used to work for me for about six months as a messenger until one day he didn't show up no more. Tall, skinny, a handsome kid with an Afro that made him look a half a foot taller than he was, which was about six feet. When he started working at the store, he was sort of nasty to everyone, including me, but then he slowly warmed up to most of the people working there. The store had a large workshop in the back where we fixed and even made jewelry. After a while, he told me he was studying the piano and hoped to get admitted to the Juilliard School of Music. We used to talk about music. I once invited him to my apartment, a couple of blocks from the store, and Miriam cooked dinner and we listened to records and I loaned him a Rubenstein long-playing.

When I called him by his name his head jerked to the side and then he twisted it around to look behind him before he realized who was calling him. Then he got all flustered and he began to shake. He looked like he was going to apologize, but he still had the knife against my neck. I held my breath.

Finally, he pulled the knife away and let it hang in his hand and he said, "I didn't know it was you." He shook his head like he was telling himself already in his young life he couldn't do nothing right.

"How's the piano coming?" I asked him.

"I'm a junkie now," he said. "My pusher works the street here, usually around Broadway, I can't find him," he said like he was explaining why he was going to rob me.

I asked him to come up to my apartment for some coffee, but he said no. He was about to leave, then he said: "Can't you loan me some money? Now that I know where you live, I'll pay you back."

I told him I only had some change with me and asked him upstairs again, telling him I'd give him money there. I wanted to sit him down and talk to him and listen to him and see what if anything, I could do to help him.

"I'll wait here," he said. "Could you loan me about twenty?"

I went upstairs and got the money. When I came back down, he was gone. I walked around the block, but all I seen were cold, lonely, two a.m. New York faces, none of which belonged to the young man who wanted to be a concert pianist.

About a month later, finally fed up with all the crime—my store was just broken into a third time—I left the city for Puerto Rico. Miriam and I had gone there a couple of times in the late 1950s, 1960. In those days, it was a paradise—for the tourists anyway. I decided I would move to Puerto Rico, to start over again, still another time.

On the day I left for Puerto Rico, it was snowing. The snowflakes were falling, large and lacey. It was beautiful, the snow falling. But I couldn't help it, I thought of ashes. I thought of ashes and of people I loved and people I lost.

ONE

Early Saturday morning and I was sitting out on the balcony of my apartment on Plaza Colón, drinking a mug of black coffee. Three cruise ships were due in and I wanted to open before the other stores to get the tourists early. In the plaza, buses were warming up and drowning out the birds chirping in the trees. A few people were sitting on benches reading newspapers, waiting for the bus drivers to open the doors to their buses. The guy who owns the small café down there was sweeping the street in front of his place.

Outside, already the sun was hot against my neck. None of the tourist shops along Calle San Francisco were open yet and there was just a few cars driving around. I passed San Francisco Church. The big wooden doors were open. Five or six people were inside, kneeling and whispering for help from their God like He's still taking part in what's going on down here.

The man with the elephant leg was sleeping on the steps of the church. His small round shaved head was resting against a concrete post. His eyes were squeezed shut like it was hurting him to sleep. His mouth was hanging open with his big bottom lip turned down. You could see the soft pink black inside and three small broken-off green things that used to be teeth. His barrel-shaped chest was quivering like there was a bird in there trying to get out.

The leg was on the bottom step, the pants torn up on one side to the thigh. It looked like a tree trunk that's got some terrible fungus disease. It's five times the regular size and there's big sores down to the puffed-up toes. His hat was sitting on its crown next to the leg. I seen tourists suddenly come across the man with the elephant leg and he would push his hat out toward them and tilt his head and croak out something and the tourists would hurry past. Some of them would have angry looks on their faces that besides the big and beautiful forts and the blue ocean and the tree-lined streets and colorful Spanish buildings they had to see this kind of sight on their vacation.

I passed the street leading down to the tourist pier. One of the liners was pulling in. As it slid closer, the gigantic white front looked like it was going to slice through the pier and move up the street, cracking through the pavement and knocking over buildings. Which of course it never did.

It would take time before the tourists got off the ship, so I stopped into La Bombonera. Strong Puerto Rican coffee bubbled in the big shiny silver Cuban coffee-making machine giving off steam behind the counter and its smell helped wake me up some more. I sat at a booth and ordered fresh orange juice, a soft-boiled egg, toast and another cup of coffee, this time half-filled with hot milk.

After a few minutes, Slatsky came in. He was wearing a starched long-sleeve white guayabera. Already the bald top of his head was shiny with sweat and the curly red hair on the sides was damp. We greeted each other and he asked: "You coming over tomorrow?"

Slatsky invites me over a couple of Sundays a month for a home-cooked meal. Then we play gin rummy, Slatsky and me against Olga's brother and his wife, who live next door. The brother is Slatsky's partner in the jewelry business. I said I'd be over. We began talking about the usual things: business and politics and the problems of everyday life, especially the latest crime and violence, which is getting worse every day. Slatsky said he was "fed up" with all the crime here and with the Latin mentality, he was moving his family next year to Israel. I didn't take him seriously, but I told him good luck. He said I should go there too. I said I was O.K. right here.

"You ain't completely accepted here, you know," Slatsky said.

I grunted. Like I been accepted every place else.

"In Israel, you'll be accepted," Slatsky said.

"It don't bother me. Who cares?" I said.

"When the *independistas start* a revolution, you'll care," Slatsky said.

"Nobody's starting no revolution," I said. "Not when there's food stamps."

"Yeah, well, you never can tell," Slatsky said. "With all the strikes and bombings they got down here, anything can happen. I got to think of my kids."

"They'll probably be on the side of the revolutionaries," I told him.

"Not *my* kids," Slatsky said.

"That's what Castro's father said."

Slatsky grunted. Then some of the other businessmen came in, including Fernández, Slatsky's brother-in-law. Fernández was over six feet tall and when he sat he always folded his hands on his huge pot belly. His eyes were covered with big sunglasses. He wore plenty of gold—an identification bracelet, a watch, rings, and chains and medals around his neck. He had a little thin mustache and a very big head with wavy black hair. He said to me: "Are you ready, my friend, to lose all your money to me tomorrow night?" He was talking about our Sunday gin rummy game, we play for nickels and dimes.

"If you think you can take it, you're welcome to it," I told him. "But don't go crying how your wife plays stupid like last time."

He pulled his big head back and let out a booming laugh. We kibitzed for another few minutes, then I left to open my store.

When I got there, I opened the safe and took out the gold jewelry and put it back behind the counter and fixed the cash register with the money from yesterday's sales. I was dusting and straightening out the chess pieces when Stevie came in.

"*Buenas dias*, Mr. Wolf. I'm almost finished with *Nostromo,* I'll return it Monday. Colonialism in Latin America. Never could happen in Puerto Rico with the U.S. as our big brother, right?" Big smile.

I grunted. "How about opening up what we got in yesterday and bringing down some stuff? Like the statues from Haiti, we need some more."

"Yeah, sure, *chévere.*" Stevie went upstairs to the stockroom.

Stevie is one of my four steady helpers. I also got one part-time on Saturdays. He's a good worker and almost never misses a day or comes late. He's what they call a Newyorican, meaning his parents are from Puerto Rico but he was born and raised in New York. He speaks a mixture of Spanish and English. He's only been in Puerto Rico a year and worked for me six months. Stevie is about twenty and got most of his education on the streets of New York. He takes courses at night at the University and I gave him some of my favorite books to read. He's got something good that many Newyoricans got. A tough spirit that ain't yet cynical. It comes from taking the best things from New York without losing the best things

ROBERT FRIEDMAN

from being Puerto Rican and all the time managing to stay in one piece in your head. That's one more way to survive when things could be against you.

Bernice hobbled in next. "How're you this morning?" she said like she says every morning with that forced smile so many Americans got, they give it no matter how they feel, like to show any other emotion but happiness was a sin. She even wears one of those smile buttons and keeps telling everyone to "have a nice day."

Bernice is hobbling because she's got a cast on her leg. She's had it there for two weeks. It's there because her husband threw her down a flight of stairs when he found her fooling around with some Puerto Rican fellow. She's got sayings and drawings and signatures all over the cast. One day a Chinaman off a boat came into the store and she's got Chinese writing down one side of the cast.

Bernice is a big woman, about thirty years old, with freckles and hair like copper wire. She ain't too bad looking except for her teeth which are long and crooked and yellowish. She's always moving out from her husband and is now living with some guy who owns a grocery store and has a wife and six kids in another home. Which is O.K. with me so long as she don't bring her problems to the store. Which ain't the case because there's always someone coming in to see her, either her angry husband or one of her boyfriends who's turned angry, and someone starts a shouting match and I get angry and kick them all out, but she always comes back with that shaky smile, all apologies, and even though I just fired her I take her back, don't ask me why because next time I ain't going to, which I told her and she knows I ain't kidding.

Bernice works behind the costume jewelry counter. I usually work the gold counter and Doris Jackson the silver counter. Stevie takes care of the stockroom and is on the floor. Don Alfonso is on the floor too and so is Carlos, the part-time helper, he also works at the University teaching a class. El Pajaro de Oro (The Golden Bird) is a good-sized store which besides jewelry has gifts and souvenirs, from the usual tourist stuff to first-class items. I've had the store for seven years now since I came down here in 1973.

Just when I opened the door for customers, Don Alfonso came in. Right behind him was Carlos. Which only left Doris Jackson, who ain't been on time more than a couple of times in all the years she's been working for me.

Don Alfonso, who's got the gout, moved slower than usual this morning, shuffling around in his starched white guayabera like he

6

was shining the floor with rags under his shoes. His high round chest, which looks like a bird's breast, and big egg-shaped head looked too heavy for his skinny bowed legs. I wanted to tell him to sit on the stool in the back until the customers started coming in, but he gets touchy and only sits there on his own. Don Alfonso is a couple of years older than me. He ain't got much hair though he's got a little goatee and what's still on top of his head is black, while I'm thick and mostly gray on top and my beard is short and grizzly.

"So how did it go last night?" I asked him.

"The usual," he said. "A few dollars won or lost, I hardly remember anymore."

We were talking about the casinos, where Don Alfonso visits practically every night. Whenever I go there, which is once or twice a week, I see him at the roulette table.

"Of course," he said, "when I was in Havana, the stakes were somewhat higher. I would win or lose thousands of dollars in a few hours at the tables. Now I am, of course, reduced to playing for peanuts. But since you are a man of the world, my friend, I'm sure you understand my predicament, that it is much easier to lose a fortune than a habit."

I grunted. Behind me, Carlos let out a loud laugh. "Again the same story of how wonderful was everything and how rich was everyone in Havana before the revolution," Carlos said. "It is really a shame that you had to surrender your fortune to Fidel before leaving Cuba so that he could spend it so foolishly on hospitals and schools for the poor."

Don Alfonso glared at Carlos. Carlos' skin was tight across his face. You could see his wide smile that showed most of his teeth wasn't really a smile. Then he said: "Here's a joke I heard yesterday. There are these two scraggily mutts that meet on Ashford Avenue. They are both owned by Cuban exiles. The first mutt says, *Hombre*, when I was living in Cuba, I had a big yard where I had my own house and I was fed steak every day, *tu sabes?* I was perfumed and my hair was tied with ribbons. I would be bathed three times a day and given big bones and I had a collar with diamonds on it. The other four-legged creature, *flaco* and mangy-looking, says, That is *nada, amigo*. When I was in Cuba, I used to be a German Shephard!"

Don Alfonso snickered. He gave Carlos a little smile and a little nod. "I appreciate the story," he said. "In fact, I will tell it to several other former German Shepherds whom I am sure will appreciate it also." Then he said, "But remember this: no matter how intelligent he may seem, a dog is only a dumb animal which lives in the world of appearances. Man, on the other hand, has little trouble distinguishing the true pedigree from the stray mongrel. The former has a definite, noble background. The latter knows neither from where it has come or to where it is going."

Whatever that meant, it meant something to Carlos. He let out a burst of sour laughter. His deep-set dark brown eyes were burning, but he smiled and talked false polite to Don Alfonso. "Excuse me, *caballero*, but may I remind you just this: the mongrel, unlike the pedigree, is a good-natured dog with a surprising intelligence which one day will help him understand his true situation. And when that day comes, when the mongrel realizes he is stronger, smarter and better in every way than the pedigree, he will rise up and attack and claim what is rightfully his."

Don Alfonso chuckled softly. Then he gave a small, confident grin, looked around at all of us and said: "I quote Don José Julián Martí, poet, patriot and great hero of the continuing Cuban fight for freedom: 'This is the age in which hills can look down on mountains'."

Carlos gave another hollow laugh and stroked his long frowning mustache. He was tall and lean and had a thin, strong-boned face mature for his age, which was about twenty-five. The maturity came from his high, always creased forehead. He suddenly tightened his mouth, widened his eyes, stuck a finger in the air and said: "The right of the fatherland to independence is not negotiable. And if it is to be negotiated, it will be with bullets. Maestro Pedro Albizu Campos."

Don Alfonso wagged a short stubby finger under Carlos' long pointed nose. "'He who serves a revolution,' he warned, 'plows the sea.' Simon Bolivar, liberator, ruler and sensible observer of his people."

"O.K.," I said, pushing between the two of them, "let's go to work, here come the customers."

Carlos glared at me. "*Yanqui* go home," he said and laughed.

The first tourists off the ships started coming in. They were mostly old people. They had on funny hats and bright shirts and baggy shorts and looked like a bunch of retired clowns who kept parts of their costumes for everyday wear.

Before I knew it, it was one-thirty and Doris Jackson still didn't show up. I called her house, but there was no answer. When Bernice came back from lunch I decided to see what the hell was the matter with Doris. She lives on the third floor of a house across from the parking garage near the post office. I went down there and I climbed the stairs, then knocked on her door. There was music from a radio or record player coming through the door and I kept knocking for five minutes till she finally answered.

"Where you been?" I said. "If you ain't coming in, why didn't you phone?"

She looked at me like she was having a hard time focusing in. Bessie, her black-and-white cat, was scooting around, hissing, then went ducking under a couch. Doris' head went backward and forward. She's fifty-something and can still be an attractive woman, but now she looked a mess. Her face was grayish, which for a Negro looks even worse than on a white person. There were all kinds of webby lines around her eyes. Her eyeballs were yellowish. She was wearing a pretty red dress, but it was wrinkled from sleeping in it. Finally, she stopped moving her head back and forth. Her voice sounded like she had been screaming at the top of her lungs the night before. I could smell the alcohol. It wasn't just coming from her breath, but off her body too.

She lowered the record player. "What time is it?" She asked like she was scared to hear the answer.

"Two o'clock," I said.

"Oh, Je-sus Christ!" she said. "Why didn't you send someone up for me earlier?" She was looking around like she had to find something right away or she would faint.

"We were too busy," I said. "I ain't going to send a special messenger just for you. What the hell is the matter with you?"

"O.K., I'm sorry. I'll be right down." She was still looking around and her body started jumping in different parts, but she didn't move from the doorway. "Damn! I can't move from this spot!" Her voice was cracking. Her face got a panicky expression until she was able to lift a leg and wiggle it.

"Will you cut it out!" I told her. "Pull yourself together."

"Oh, my God, what the hell am I doing? I'm killing myself."

She began to cry.

I was getting angry, but I stopped myself. I been through this with her before. Too many times before. I could see inside to part of her living room and the rest of it came into view inside my head: the polished black-and-white tile floor, the new-looking rattan furniture, the big straw peacock chair painted white, the Picasso reproductions in frames on the walls, the tall, full bookcase. Everything neat and clean and in place. Just like her life wasn't. Go figure,

"Christ, I'm ruining my goddamn life!" Tears rolled down her cheeks. She opened her mouth and twisted her face but she wasn't making any sounds.

"Go back to bed," I said. "Rest up and I'll see you Monday." I was trying to be nice. Because when you've tried everything else to help a person, there ain't nothing else left to be. Still, her helplessness irritated me.

Her left eyelid started snapping down and up, down and up like it was sending Morse code. "Shit, I got that tic again!"

"You're a pain in the ass," I told her. She nodded. I left. The woman on the record player, her voice I remembered was Billie Holiday, started singing again.

I usually get my lunch brought to the store. But this time, I walked around until I reached La Mallorquina and sat at the counter and ordered a ham and cheese on a toasted *mallorca*, and I had another coffee with hot milk.

Larry Cruz came into the restaurant. He looked around, seen me and came up to the counter.

"Dzién dobrey, Pan Wolf," he said. He tapped the stool beside me. *Czy mogę?"*

He asked if he could sit next to me. I liked this guy. He always greeted me in Polish, which he told me he learned from Polish-American buddies in the Army.

We met when he came into my store to buy a birthday present for his wife, it was a silver bracelet I made. We talked and I learned he was a printmaker, he made posters for the government, along with his other artwork, He had been in the Army, fighting in the jungles in Viet Nam. His wife, Betty, taught English and Spanish in Central High School in Santurce.

Larry Cruz carried a copy of the *San Juan Star* and we both looked at the headline about Los Macheteros killing two U.S. sailors outside a Naval base here, supposedly to revenge some fellow revolutionary who was found hanged in his cell in a jail in Florida. I suppose the terrorists (some people call them freedom fighters) saw this as helping get independence for the island, but I was irritated by lots of things and I said that killing those two sailors was just a bunch of bullshit. I expected some sort of something or other from Larry Cruz because he wants Puerto Rico to be its own country, which I could understand. If you know anything about the history of Lithuania or Poland, they also had to keep fighting to be independent. He nodded and didn't argue with me. Then he said: "You don't kill as a symbolic act."

I agreed. You only kill the killers themselves.

I went back to my store. We got some more tourists off the boats, then closed at six. That was just the first half of my day.

TWO

Stevie spent most of the day in the stock room unpacking cartons. Wrapped inside the carton from a workshop in the mountains that crafted Taino Indian items were necklaces, earrings, and bracelets decorated with lots of straight and curving lines and dots inside circles surrounded by circles, symbolizing snails, frogs, birds, shamans, the sun. There were three-pointed stone *cemis* you could hold in your hand. The *cemis,* which had carved faces on one end, supposedly represented Taino deities and ancestral spirits

"So what did they teach in school in New York about the Tainos?"

Carlos had come upstairs, supposedly to give Stevie a hand in getting the newly arrived merchandise downstairs and shelved.

"Not much," said Stevie.

Carlos gave his wide, somehow joyless smile. "Why am I not surprised? You probably learned about Apollo and Zeus and Neptune and Venus, all those Greeks and Romans, but did they teach you about *Yocahu,* the Supreme Taino god, and *Jurakán,* the God of guess what kind of storm? Did they at least mention all the *caciques*, who happened to be the rulers of the land like all the Louies of France and the kings of England, but much more sane than, say, Louis XIV or George III, the nut who lost the U.S. because even way back then, the leaders of the village tribes were the guys with the most followers—and their kids didn't inherit their gold and feather headdresses. It went to the next guy with the biggest clan. Sounds something like Democracy, huh? So the Spanish, of course, had to kill them all off.

"What else didn't you learn in the schools there about our island before it became a 'tourist playground'? Did you learn that it only took the Spaniards 50 years to wipe out all our forefathers? How about the Treaty of Paris, when the U.S. got us as 'war booty'? Were you taught that the big U.S. companies took over our farmland, so we couldn't grow our food, that U.S. corporations made a killing by taking over our sugar plantations, that all the kids in our schools were forced to learn everything in English for about 50 years, until they realized in Washington that we were going to continue speaking Spanish, whether they liked it or not? I'm sure the gringo educators pointed out to your young mind that since we weren't considered smart enough, we had to have a governor sent down from the states to run our political lives until the United Nations told the U.S. to get rid of its colonies and Washington came up with that phony thing called 'commonwealth,' which anyone who knows anything, knows it's just another word for colony."

Stevie started for the staircase leading down to the store. "I got to get these downstairs."

"Yeah, wait a minute. I just want to know what they teach you guys up in New York. Did you learn that our U.S. citizenship, which we got in 1914, just in time for our young guys to be drafted for the First World War and all Uncle Sam's other Great Wars, but still doesn't allow us here to vote in Congress or for the wonderful president who decides to send our guys to kill and get killed? And what about the great economic program that lets gringo business owners operate factories here without paying taxes because they're creating so many jobs on the island, even though the 'official' unemployment rate is 20 percent, and probably closer to 40 percent, and more than half of the people living here can't afford to buy their food, unless they get government food stamps. Did you learn that we import practically all our food from the U.S. which we can only get by U.S. ships that charge much more than other flagships, then go into U.S.-owned supermarkets that boost the price even more for food? Were you taught that . . . ?"

"I'm gonna bring some of these boxes downstairs," Stevie said.

He slowly set out the crafts on their assigned shelves. No, P.S. 88 and Evander Childs High weren't strong on the history of the island. But he'd heard through relatives and read in books a lot of those things that the island and the people had been through.

Sure, Puerto Ricans had been treated lousy down through the years—both on the island and in the states. He should feel for them, for us. Wasn't he a "spic?" Yeah, sure—sort of—even though he had been in the states for almost all his life. He was a New York kid, as American as any other Yankee fan. No, he was a PR, look at that sort of olive skin, made pale from the cold. But no, not quite because for the people here, his gringo-accented Spanish made him an "Americano."

So. Fuck it—he was what he was.

Stevie reluctantly returned to the stock room, and Carlos immediately picked up his narrative.

"While I'm sure you weren't taught about *El Grito de Lares,* our first Revolution against the Spaniards who took over our home, yet I'll bet your Hebe teachers filled you with propaganda about how the Jews deserved to take away land from the Arabs for the creation of Israel and your Mick teachers told you all about the Easter Uprising of 1916 in Dublin, Ireland, but didn't teach you about the influence that revolt had on our independence movement and how the fuckin' FBI fucked up the movement by arresting anyone brave enough to say Puerto Rico should be its own country. How our true father, Don Pedro Albizu Campos, was influenced by the leaders of the Dublin uprising. Did you get any lessons on how both Albizu in Puerto Rico and James Connolly in Ireland were great defenders of the working class and organized strikes and used those strikes and the labor movements to create Nationalist movements and both planned insurrections against their oppressors? Yeah, you probably heard about the Easter Rising of 1916, but did they teach you about the Nationalist Insurrection of Jayuya in 1950? You should have been taught that Connolly stressed the Catholicism of the Irish as a means of creating a clear cultural separation from the Protestant British, just as Albizu stressed the Catholicism of Puerto Rico and the Protestantism of the U.S. as a way of showing our different values. Values that the U.S. was trying to eradicate in Puerto Rico."

"O.K.," Stevie said. "I get the idea."

Carlos pulled his long, narrow head back and laughed. "Yeah, yeah," he said. "So here's my plan. We—meaning, of course, those of us serious about gaining independence for Puerto Rico—on the next Good Friday, we take over the main U.S. Post Office, just down the block in Old San Juan. All the post offices in Puerto Rico are closed on Good Friday because, see, we are a Catholic majority. So there will be just a few guards in or around the building who we can easily subdue. We tell the media what will be going down just a few minutes before we do the takeover, which should be bloodless. We break through the front doors and go to the second-floor balcony, where we hang the flag of Puerto Rico and declare the Republic of

Puerto Rico. We announce that we will not leave or allow anyone in the building until the U.S. agrees to sign a pact we will draw up guaranteeing our independence and freedom and that we freedom fighters are not punished for our actions. We sure as hell will make news in the U.S., not to mention the rest of the world.

"So, I'm recruiting young idealistic guys to carry out the Good Friday Uprising. You seem to be an idealistic guy. You don't have to give me an answer now. Think about it. We'll talk more later."

Another joyless smile, this time accompanied by a wink. Was Carlos kidding him? Kidding himself? Who the hell knew who was doing what or would be doing on the crazy political scene here.

Stevie started unpacking boxes of lovely, bright-colored Haitian paintings. He couldn't wait for the day to be over so he could home to his novel about the cabin boy traveling around the world.

The confusion and guilt, whatever the hell he was feeling, grabbed, hit hardest and weakened him most as he was walking the few blocks from the store to his apartment. Of course, Carlos' idea—the Good Friday takeover of the post office—was . . . what? Ridiculous? Crazy? Brilliant? All the above?

Well, let's see: Where the hell did Stevie Díaz stand on . . . certain things? Puerto Rico should be its own country, he believed that. Then he would fit in much better—wherever.

He was going to travel the world with Fico, via his Olivetti 22.

Still, he wanted to know where the hell he stood here and now—in his heart as well as in his head.

THREE

When I got home I tried to nap, but even though I had so little sleep the night before I couldn't fall asleep. I had this hard-tight ball in my stomach. I almost always got it, but most of the time I don't pay it no attention. But sometimes it presses in on me. Like it was doing then. I read a little. I listened to my Mozart records. I made myself tea. I ate another ham and cheese sandwich. Then I showered and put on a suit and tie and went to the casinos.

First, I went to the Caribe Hilton. It was so crowded, I couldn't get a table. Don Alfonso was playing roulette there. He was jiggling a small pile of chips in his hands, betting one or two at each spin of the wheel. A little smile was curled up in the corner of his mouth like he was making fun of himself because of his small bets. He didn't see me and I didn't greet him.

I went to the Condado and got a seat at the blackjack table in a casino there, between a lady with three chins that shook every time she lost a hand, and a little bald guy with a smelly cigar, he kept dropping ashes on the table. Soon the lady lost all her chips and got up to leave and I took her seat at the end of the table. When you're the last to be dealt you got the most influence on the dealer's hand. Once, I had fifteen and the dealer had a nine showing. I drew another card and it was an eight. The dealer had a five under the nine then drew a seven for twenty-one. If I didn't take that last card, the dealer would have got stuck with the eight and gone over and everyone at the table would have won. As it was, we all lost. Everyone started grumbling and the bald guy blew smoke in my face and said, "You shouldn't have hit, my friend."

One thing that gets me mad is stupidity making believe it knows what it's talking about. "Shut up what you don't know about," I told him.

"What are you talking?" he said. His cigar was jumping around in his mouth like it was looking for a fight.

I didn't say nothing. I wasn't going to explain that when you got fifteen and the dealer's got nine showing, you ask for a hit when you're counting cards and you know the odds are that he's got a picture card underneath for nineteen.

But still, with everything I know about blackjack, even though I was over two hundred dollars ahead earlier, by the time the casinos closed at four in the morning, I lost it all back, plus another hundred. Sometimes it ain't enough to know. In cards, and everything else.

When I got outside I realized I was hungry so I took a cab to an all-night restaurant on Luna Street, a couple of blocks from where I live. The place was crowded with guys dressed like girls, drug addicts, pimps, pushers, old prostitutes. I ordered a Spanish omelet and coffee. Some guy in dark-lensed glasses sat at a table across from me, taking deep puffs from a cigarette and tipping the ashes into the coffee cup across from him. He had a pale face like he never went out in the daylight, and a tight, mean mouth.

I didn't look at him no more until a girl who came out of the ladies' room and sat across from him yelled: *"Pendejo!* You put ashes in my coffee, I ain't finished it yet."

I recognized the voice. It was Carmen. She got up and went to the counter to get some more coffee. On her way back, she saw me. Her little face, which looked tired and drawn, broke into a smile. She started over to the table. Her eyes were big and shiny.

"Ay, Papi,'s good t' see jou." She was slurring her words more than usual. "Come on, sit o'er here. I wan' you should meet Manny."

I didn't feel like meeting no Manny. I told her I already ordered some food.

"Don' matter," she said. "Come on." She was wobbling and her coffee was spilling. I took the cup from her and brought it to the other table and decided to sit for a few minutes.

Carmen said, "Manny, this is Mr. Wolf I tol' you about. He's good people, you know? And this is Manny. He's my pusher."

Manny's head shot forward. "She don't know what she's talking," he said. "I'm her cousin from Bayamon."

"Si, hombre, you my cousin. And you my pusher too. He gets me the dope, you know? You don't got to worry about Mr. Wolf. He don' care what you into."

Manny sat back and put a hand under his chin. He looked at Carmen like he was trying to decide the best way to cripple her. He had black curly hair and little holes in his face. His mouth was real tight.

Then he threw his head back and let out a laugh like it was coming from a machine gun. "You're too much, you know, baby," he said.

Carmen smiled sweetly. It was a slow peaceful thing spreading over her lips.

Her eyes started to close and her head dropped slowly to her chest, then bobbed up again, then slid down to her chest again.

I first met Carmen after I came one night from the casino at the El San Juan Hotel. She was outside the hotel where I was playing blackjack.

When I saw her I didn't want nothing to do with her. She looked too young and so skinny she would break in two if you touched her. But she came up to me and started talking with a big smile. She had a thin pretty face with soft black dreamy eyes and long black hair. When she got up close you could see she wasn't no teenager. I told her she looked like she needed a good meal, so I bought her some chicken and rice at a restaurant on Isla Verde Avenue. While we were eating she asked me where I lived and when I told her she said she lived near me, could I give her a ride. Then inside the taxi she asked could she come up to my apartment, we'll have a good time, but I said I was tired, maybe some other time.

Two nights later, she knocked on the door of my apartment about three in the morning. I had showed her the building where I lived when I took her home and we both got out of the cab at the Plaza Colon. She said she looked on the mailboxes downstairs for my name which I told her the night we met, then saw a light under my door.

I usually get a couple hours sleep after I close my store at six, take a long, fast walk for an hour, eat something, then stay up late. I been writing the book about my life, *The Autobiography of a Non-Famous Man*, which I started writing when I first came down here from New York seven years ago. It'll be finished when I'm finished. Sometimes I'm up late making jewelry. I work with silver. Or I may be painting. I got a couple of styles. One is like Chagall, only stronger. I got more hate inside me. I also do paintings and collages that's got wheels and gears in them. Like the Italian Futurists, but without the fascism. I believe in machines. Why not? You use them for good, they make a better world. If you make things with your hands, you got to admire what a machine can do.

Anyway, Carmen said she carne up to see me because her brother was after her with a knife, could she stay awhile. Only she didn't look too scared. She had a sleepy smile on her lips and a look in her eyes like they were focusing in on some other planet.

I was gonna tell her to go to the police, but she looked so out of the world, I let her come in. So she stumbles into my apartment and takes off her clothes and says she'll have sex with me for twenty dollars. Her arms were like broomsticks, and I saw the marks there, and the skinny little girl's legs with a black-and-blue mark the size of a grapefruit on her thigh. And her titties, they almost ain't there. She took off a large crucifix she wore on a silver chain around her neck and put it on the dresser, face down, so He don't have to see what would be going on.

I was ready to give her the twenty dollars and send her back out. She sat on the edge of the bed and lit a cigarette and her head started bobbing like it was on strings. The cigarette fell from her hand. I picked it up and gave it to her and she looked up and said with a dreamy smile, "*Gracias*, Papi."

She dropped the cigarette again and this time I picked it up and put it out. "Get dressed and get the hell out of here," I told her.

But she didn't hear a word. She was fast asleep, all twisted up like she was in a strange shaped womb. I was gonna shake her, but she looked so out of it, I put a sheet over her skinny naked body and put out the light and slept on the sofa.

She's been back several times in the past few weeks. I let her in, who the hell knows why? A couple of times I lent her money when she was real desperate. I knew she spent it on drugs. She once asked for ten dollars and I gave it to her and she kept thanking me and said she was going to buy her little sister medicine and I got mad and grabbed the ten dollars back. She didn't make up no lies after that. Sometimes she came over and surprised me by not asking for nothing, but just sat on my balcony. We would sit out there on unraveling straw chairs and Carmen would talk about when she was a little girl living in the countryside, saying she wished she could have stayed ten years old. And I'd think of my daughter Rachel when she was eight, which was the last year of her life.

Carmen would remember riding horses up and down the mountains and she'd remember eating coconut molasses candy and go on about the things she did when she was a kid. Then she'd get real quiet and the copper-colored skin on her little face would get pinched over her high cheekbones and her small round mouth would shrivel into itself and her dark eyes would look heavy. You knew she wasn't remembering good things then. Then she'd flash me a smile and get up from the chair like an old lady and say she had to do some "shopping" (buy drugs). Sometimes I just let her sleep over, in my bed, I took the sofa.

Like I said, who the hell knows why.

Now this Manny was shaking his head. "What a crazy bitch," he said. "Hey, where you from, Mr. Wolf?"

I told him I was from too many places. He nodded like he understood.

"You from New York too?"

I nodded.

"Yeah, man," he said. "I was brought up in El Barrio, you know, Spanish Harlem. Then we moved to Brooklyn, till they tore down the neighborhood. Then to the Bronx. I lived on Simpson Street, you know where that is? The South Bronx, that's where I left to come here. What a shithole that place is now! Goddamn. PRs living in garbage up there, man. Disgusting! Hey, you Jewish?"

I grunted.

"I don't know what's the matter with the PRs, they can't get it together like the Jews and help themselves out of the *mierda*. Yeah, I really admire the Jews, man. They look out for each other. That's what the Ricans got to do. They got to get organized and look out for their own and fuck the rest that get in the way. Like what the Jews do. I really admire them for doing that. Aw, forget about New York now, man. It's a drag, you can't live there no more. Not with all them fuckin' junkies and sickies running around. That's why I come back here. I got a two-year-old kid and I don't want her growing up with all them degenerates around. Bad news, that fuckin' city."

Carmen's head shot up. "Sí, Manolo," she said. "You right, baby. When I come back here, I bring my little sister wit' me. I don' want her hanging out wit' all them junkies."

"So where she at now," Manny said. "With you and your pimp brother down in La Perla, right? So that's better for her? You and your brother ain't all the time shooting up in the house?"

"We family, baby," Carmen said. She made a face like something was hurting then got up to take another trip to the bathroom. The waiter brought my omelet and coffee.

Manny shook his head. He made a disgusted expression with his mouth. "Jesus, ain't that bitch somethin' else? You know, Mr. Wolf, a junkie ain't got no sense. They can't figure things out like you and me. Something happens in their head from all that dope. They can't think right, you can't believe 'em, you can't trust 'em, and after a while you don't even want to look at 'em. They're disgusting man. *La verdad.* That's the truth."

I looked at him like he was a bug and his face got a little red.

"Hey, I know what I'm talking about. I been there, you know?" he said. "I used to be hooked myself. But I got smart and kicked years ago. I got to make a living, you know? So I'm in the business I know best. Just like you, I bet, right? We all got to do what we know best. I make good money. Why shouldn't I? I'm bringing my kid up by myself. Her mother's a junkie, she ain't worth shit. Believe me, I know what I'm talking about. I been there and back. We all got to do our thing, man."

I felt the veins by my temple pulsing. I was going to pick up the salt shaker and throw it at this Manny when a guy-girl in a low cut red silk dress came running from the ladies' room up to the table. The person had pink hair puffed out like cotton candy and huge brown bulging eyes with eyelashes like the legs of a large insect. There was dark mascara around the eyes, a little rhinestone on the side of the nose and lips like red wax. The face was wide with puffy cheeks, they looked like cotton was stuffed in them, and it was twitching all over and the mouth was babbling to Manny: *"Mira, corazón,* you bitch is in there and the door was open by the booth and she sittin' on the potty with her eyes wide like somethin' biting her on the ass and her arm is hangin' down and right in the middle there she got the needle stickin' out of it and her face is all blue, then she starts falling off the potty, I put her down on the ground. I think that bitch is OD-ing, you better go and see."

"For Christ *fuckin'* sake!" Manny said. He got up and went into the ladies' room. Half a dozen others followed him in.

They came out a couple of minutes later, Carmen being carried over Manny's shoulder. He let her down in a chair. She wasn't blue no more. She was more a gray color.

She started sliding off the chair and Manny grabbed an arm and yanked her up on her feet and slapped her hard twice across the cheek. Her eyes still didn't open. Then, with Manny holding her right arm, she started tilting to the left. He yanked her up straight again.

"Wake up, bitch!" he shouted into Carmen's face. "Wake up, or you're gonna be dead!"

Carmen stayed unconscious.

"Walk her, walk her," several people were shouting.

Manny looked around. He had an expression on his face like he was trying to decide something. Then he yanked Carmen over to me.

"You walk her, Wolf," he said. "You better wake her or it's all over. I got to get home before my kid gets up. I'm sorry, man, but that's it." He pushed Carmen at me and walked out of the restaurant.

I jumped up and caught her. I put her in a chair again and she started falling out of it till a couple of other people ran over and picked her up onto her feet. I ran out of the restaurant, the sides of my temples pounding. I started running down the street and caught up to Manny and grabbed his shoulder and spun him around. He flew back against a parked car. He looked surprised as hell.

"Get the hell back there, you sonovabitch, and take care of your own goddamn problems!" I hollered.

"That bitch ain't *my* problem," Manny said. "She's her own fuckin' problem."

I moved closer to him ready to pull him off the car. I was so angry, I was feeling dizzy. "What kind of animal are you?" I said.

Manny put a hand in his pants pocket. "This kind." He pulled out a little black gun and pointed it at me. "Now get the fuck out of the way motherfucker before I blow your fuckin' head off!"

I couldn't see his eyes behind the dark glasses, but I was sure there was murder in them. His face was sickly white with a scarlet gash for a mouth. I backed away. He nodded slowly, telling me I made the right move. He whistled through his teeth for a taxi coming up the street. "Nice meeting you, Mr. Wolf."

He gave the machine gun cackle again, got in the taxi and it sped away.

My whole body was shaking. I ran back to the restaurant. Carmen was propped up in a chair and held there by two fat hookers while the guy in the red silk dress was slapping and shaking her. Then the two hookers lifted her under the arms and walked her around and then the guy in the dress slapped her and shook her some more, and then they walked her again. I sat watching as they slapped her and shook her and walked her. Finally, she unglued her eyelids and seemed to be coming around. They walked her around some more, then gave her some coffee. She sipped it slowly while someone held the cup for her.

I went up to her and she seen me and tried to smile.

"You O.K. now?" I asked.

"She sat there with a little smile like someone just whispered a small secret in her ear. Then she tried to say something, but it was so weak I couldn't hear it.

"I think she going to be O.K. now," said the guy in the red silk dress. I nodded and turned to go. All of a sudden, I was tired as hell. Then Carmen called out to me in a weak voice, "Papi, don' go, don' go." She still had the little smile on her face. "Let's go outside, O.K.?" She got up like she was a hundred years old and took hold of my arm.

We walked slow up to, then along the street above La Perla. The mist over the green tarpaper roofs glistened in the street lamps down there. You could smell the ocean, it was black and quiet like a cat ready to pounce, and then waves broke, you could hear them pounding below. Carmen was quiet. She kept holding my arm and yawning. We stopped when we got to a flight of steps cut into the high wall that separates La Perla from the rest of the Old City. Carmen leaned over the wall and looked down at the houses and shacks huddled below.

She let out a deep sigh. "I don't wanna go down there now," she said. "My brudder, he's gonna gibe me a whole lotta chit. Can I stay wit' you tonight?" Her face was drawn and pinched like a little old lady's face. She looked ready to fall off her feet again.

I took a deep deep breath. "O.K.," I said. "Come on."

I took her arm and we went down the hill to Plaza Colón then across the street to my apartment.

I told her to sleep in my bed, I would sleep on the couch, but she wanted me to be in the bed with her. She took my arm and put it around her shoulders and put her head on my chest and soon was asleep. Her little pinched face twitched. Then her lips flattened and her eyebrows went up like she was finding her dream hard to believe. Then she shrugged and started snoring.

She turned on her side and her hair fell across her cheek and her neck. Like Sarah, my first wife. She turned again and her mouth opened slightly and she let out a long sigh; then she drew in air with two gasps like she suddenly realized something crucial was about to escape with the long breath. Her mouth closed and her face began to relax and she looked innocent of what she and life had made of each other.

Then I thought: I want to protect her, and something warm came over the numbness that's inside me and it made me shiver. And I kept shivering.

FOUR

What the hell is the matter with me?

Doris Jackson poured the rest of the rum into a glass, downed it, tossed the bottle into the garbage can under the sink. She swore she would give it up—for the next couple of days.

Billie sang:

> "Rich relations give
> "Crust of bread and such
> "You can help yourself
> "But don't take too much
> "Mama may have, Papa may have
> "But God bless the child
> "That's got his own

Doris joined in:

> "He's got his owwwwn."

Oh, Billie, I could listen to you day and night, drunk or sober. Ella and Sarah are great, so was little Maxine Sullivan, big Mildred Bailey, Alberta, Betty Carter. And, of course, Bessie, who I never saw. She surely comes through on her records. Still, Lady Day—no one like Miss Holiday.

Doris Jackson had tried, just out of high school. Gigs around hometown Cleveland. Good write-ups, even in the *Plain-Dealer*. Gave it a go in New York. Small clubs down in the Village, up in Harlem. Sang one night at that club in Sugar Hill. She almost fainted when Coleman Hawkins joined her and the trio in her last set. Still, she had the guts to sing *Body and Soul* with the Hawk riffing in the background. He congratulated her. Heaven, she was in heaven!

She almost made it. But she didn't.

No drugs. Just drink.

Then there was John Jackson, the sonovabitch who if he didn't drive her to drink, certainly pushed her to step on the gas.

He wasn't a complete sonovabitch, Doris. You know that. You loved the bastard—even when you hated him. Not possible? Well, it was for that crazy Doris Jackson.

A couple of years of secretarial studies—shorthand, typing, accounting, billing, records management, telecommunications, etc., etc. Very good student, when sober, Aunt Maude pushed her to apply as a court clerk. Steady job, good salary. She was living near Sugar Hill, still singing on some weekends. Met some guys, mostly musicians. A short affair, here and there.

Then, John Jackson.

She was at her desk in the clerks' office, New York County Courthouse, also known as New York State Supreme Court, 60 Centre St., Foley Square, when he rushed in, flapping the *amicus curiae* brief, demanding to file it immediately, since he had a hearing at the federal courthouse down the street in five minutes. Doris went to the counter to give a hand out of the goodness (and somewhat speeded-up beating of) her heart for the tall, handsome, mustached, black-haired hunk. He was filing the papers on behalf of the NAACP? The Urban League?—she didn't remember—in a suit against the New York Police Department for beating into unconsciousness a 16-year-old black kid.in some phony drug case (pot, pills) involving the kid buying the drugs from an undercover agent. John Jackson's eyes said, "Hey, babe, that kid could have been your younger brother."

She helped him and two hours later, just before she was going home, he was back, pearly teeth and a sort-of phony searching with his lovely deepest brown eyes. Did he leave his pen here? Damn! It was a Vintage Parker 51, a gift from his aunt Billie. Billie Holiday? No, he laughed. Wilhelmina Jackson, his father's older sister. He had the pen for years, since graduating from NYU law school.

No pen. Damn! Anyway, he said, as though it shouldn't be a total loss, let's go for a drink. She went for a drink. And dinner. And to his apartment in the Village. (He actually had the one and only Billie's records.) And to his bed.

Love came to Doris Jackson.

A couple of months later, marriage. Her first, his second. He had two kids from the first marriage. He was a damn lawyer, he said, but he wound up paying much too much for the kids' support.

Still, he loved his kids and figured that the bitch (wife one) was spending the support check on her own goddamn self.

Five months later, a stillborn for Doris. They would try again, she was assured. He wanted his love for her, John Jackson said, spawned in the material form of their child.

That's swell, thought Doris. But the second child never materialized.

Still, the Village in the late Fifties and the Sixties. The Beats. The Hippies. Walking to work at the courthouse on warm days. Eating out practically every night at wonderful restaurants. Best of all, Miles, Trane, Monk, MJQ—she even saw Billie down there once. At a movie theater in Sheridan Square. They wouldn't let Billie appear in night clubs in New York. Like she was the only entertainer on drugs. She came from a gig in Philadelphia, arriving after midnight. She started off wobbly, then got into her groove. *God, was she great!*

Then, somewhere along the way, the beatings began. Of course, she deserved them! You see, besides not doing exactly as she was told, what she did would purposely piss him off and screw everything up—from pouting her lips at those other guys at their table during the Bar Association dinner like she wanted to give them all blow jobs, to losing the key to their apartment—he left his home—after a long night of boozing at some night club and having to wake the under-his-breath-cursing super. And just drinking too damn much! Almost as much as he did! She moved out. He begged her to move back in. She moved back in. He knew she wanted him to whack her around again. So he did. They split. Got together. Finally, out of New York, down to Puerto Rico, to live and let live.

She got a saleswoman job at the jewelry-souvenir store a couple of blocks from where she found an apartment in Old San Juan. She stopped drinking, for a while.

Wolf, the owner of the store, a Jewish man from Europe, he made it through the war. He was lucky, he said, that he wasn't turned into a lampshade. Not too funny, but when he wasn't complaining about things, he was really nice to be around. He was intelligent and he loved Mozart and Doris lent him Billie records and he said things about her singing that showed he understood what she was singing, about the hurt and the feeling and the love and the sadness and even happiness that comes through. He lent Doris books, introduced her to Thomas Mann and Dostoyevsky and to painters he loved like Rembrandt because what he showed you made you feel what was way deep inside, and Goya because he knew the face of cruelty and beauty too. When she came down to Puerto Rico, she was in her late forties and she already felt like an old woman. Wolf didn't seem to have any age, her excuse for sleeping with him. Which she did in those early years and could even have been in love with the guy, who made her laugh and made her smarter.

Then—goddamnit!—John Jackson arrived in Puerto Rico. He found where she lived through Sylvia, his sister, who Doris still kept in contact with, thinking Sylvia was on Doris's side, which evidently, she made believe she was but really wasn't.

So contrite he was, so apologetic, so sweet, so generous—until that night at *La Boutella,* the Old City nightclub.

They sat at the bar and listened to that woman singing and accompanying herself on the piano—Renee Arden, a lovely little blues-tinted voice. She twirled in her seat to watch the singer, applauded, twirled back to the bar, then, several more times, back to Renee, the bar, the entertainer.

When they got back to her apartment, where stupid she let him stay the night, he said: "Hey, bitch, why the fuck at your age are you still wearing a miniskirt? Was it so's you could keep opening your fuckin' legs on the barstool so all those horny PRs could get a good look up there? I seen them looking up there. Just what you wanted, right, bitch? You're a whore and this is what you deserve."

The slaps across her face came fast and loud, then the punches began, in her stomach, then in the eye, and the hair pulled until she was on the ground, trying to kick her way free.

Then he left the apartment and, she found out later, slept on a bench in the Plaza Colón. The day after, she was delivered a pair of diamond earrings from the Jewels of the World store on Fortaleza Street. "So sorry," was the message on the card inside the jewelry box.

He disappeared, for six months, came to the island, begged, begged, *begged* her forgiveness and, well . . .

Goddamn! What a jackass you are, Doris!

Doris Jackson looked into her refrigerator, pulled out some tomato juice, drank from the bottle.

Goddamn if she wouldn't change! Become her own person!

She wished she had another bottle or rum somewhere so she could smash it to pieces.

After pouring herself just one more.

She went back into the living room, sat on her white-painted straw peacock chair, legs stretched out and crossed, Bessie was out from under the couch, licking her paws. As Doris continued figuring ways to put her life back together, Bessie looked up, shaking her head, telling Doris it didn't matter what she told herself, mothing would change.

No, no! She would turn it around. Dig herself out, return to the brief good times. Back to her truest loves.

Goddamn, she would!

FIVE

I got up with the sun. I showered, dressed and went downstairs to buy a newspaper. I made myself breakfast and read the paper, then started on a painting. It was going to be a portrait. The woman I started sketching with a pencil on the canvas had two sides to her face. She was Carmen, but Sarah too,

Carmen didn't get out of bed until the afternoon. She came into the back room where I do my painting. She looked weak and shaky. She went into the kitchen and had some coffee. She came back after a while and looked better. I had her sit and pose for a while, then realized it wasn't necessary, the whole thing had to come out of my head. She watched me drawing and painting and then she said: "I finished with the dope, Papi. Last night was the last time."

"That's good," I said. I looked over to her. "I hope you ain't fooling yourself."

"I ain't foolin'. I'm off that shit now." She gave me a big warm smile. Then she said: "I wanna stay here. O.K., Papi? You come home from work and I'm gonna make you dinner. I gonna do the laundry too. And water the plants. And other t'ings too." She ran her tongue slowly across her top lip. I seem enough hookers do that and I got angry. But what the hell, she did what she know. So I took her to bed and we used our tongues on each other. Then I went inside her, angry, but grateful too.

After, she hugged me and kissed me and looked deep at me and I told her she could stay for a while and I felt better about it than I thought I would. She was as good as her word and cooked me dinners, *asapaos* (chicken and shrimp stews) and fresh fish she bought from fishermen down by the docks. We made love and

I felt something opening up inside me like a flower in a speeded-up movie. I felt like a young man again. Almost.

I postponed the visit to Slatsky's. Then the next week I told him I had a guest staying with me, could I bring her over on the coming Sunday? Slatsky said O.K. He didn't ask any questions. He's a good guy.

Slatsky lives in a high-rise condominium on Ashford Avenue in the Condado section. His penthouse apartment looks over the ocean and he pays plenty for it. But he's got plenty from two jewelry stores he already owns in the Old City and the jewelry factory he's got an interest in in another part of San Juan. Slatsky's got a good life. Olga, his Cuban wife, is still a good-looking woman in her early fifties and she cooks wonderful. The twins, Richie and Tommy, are Slatsky's pride and joy, and his daughter, Lisa, who's already in high school, is turning into a beauty and gets A's in all her subjects.

Like I said, Slatsky is a good man. He's the person I feel closest to down here. I met him on the day I opened my store here. He visited as a representative of the Old San Juan Merchants Association to welcome me, and ask me to join the organization, which I did, paying my yearly dues right away. I was wearing a short-sleeved white shirt and Slatsky seen the numbers. He rolled up the long-sleeved shirt he was wearing and showed me his numbers.

"Birkenau" he said.

I said: "Auschwitz 1."

We didn't discuss it further in all the years of our friendship in Puerto Rico.

The difference between us is that deep down Slatsky is mostly grateful, but I ain't. He's grateful for being able to live normal again and he wants to keep on living that way. He's a leader at the synagogue here and is always donating to charities.

I'm glad I'm still alive too. But I ain't giving thanks to nobody or nothing down here or "up there."

The dinner, *ropa vieja*, which is stewed beef, vegetables, tomatoes, onion, etc., was delicious and we drank red wine from Spain. Everyone was happy around the table. talking about the tourists who would come into the shops and say they didn't change their dollars into Puerto Rican money, could they still buy something? Or about the local politicians, they\'re always doing crazy things like the mayor of some town out on the island who asked for money from the government so he could investigate the flying saucers everyone in the town, including him, was seeing. That was the good part of the night. But there was other parts that weren't so good. Like when the new doorman stopped me and Carmen from going into the building and asked where we were going. He was nasty like we weren't good enough to be there. I told him it was none of his business where we were going and we got into an argument until Slatsky's daughter Lisa came home from a friend's house and told him who I was. He grunted like he still didn't believe we were respectable enough to be visiting there. As we went to the elevator, I saw me and Carmen in a long mirror. She was wearing the same clothes for the whole week, washing them out each night: purple shorts, a gold-colored blouse, lime-colored turban, pink platform shoes and big round gold earrings. My shirt and pants were creased and my hair was flying around my head and there were dark circles under my eyes. Maybe the doorman had a point.

Carmen was quiet most of the night, smiling at everyone. She only started getting fidgety towards the end when we played cards and Olga and the kids watched TV. She kept moving from the card table where she sat behind me to watch me play, to the sofa where she joined the TV watching. I knew she was getting bored and restless, and maybe something more, but she didn't say nothing.

After the first few minutes of shock, of seeing me bring someone to the house which I never done before, let alone Carmen, everyone was very nice to her.

Everyone, except Fernández. He kept saying half-kidding things to her and winking at the rest of us. He asked her if she was a gypsy and if she told fortunes and could she read his palm. Carmen just smiled.

After the card game, the kids went to bed and Olga served coffee and cake. We all sat around the kitchen table, and Fernández launched into his favorite topic. Which was about how him and his Cuban exile friends were going to invade Cuba and free it from Fidel Castro and Communism. Every Sunday he brings this up. Fernández is a veteran of the Bay of Pigs invasion, he was captured then let go, and now he's an official in one of the exile groups that's always talking about trying again.

"We are finalizing the plans," he told us real serious. He had finished his coffee and cake and his hands were folded on his huge belly. His black silk shirt was open to just above his navel. He had two gold chains around his neck. "And this time," he said, "there is no President Kennedy to pull out our air cover at the last minute. This time we will reach the mountains, as Fidel had done, and take back that which is ours. This time we will succeed." He leaned forward and smacked his fist on the table and the coffee cups and spoons rattled and a spoon jumped off the table. Olga picked it up.

Nobody said nothing. Slatsky once told me that both Olga and Fernández 's wife were satisfied with their lives in Puerto Rico. Both got it better here than they ever had it in Cuba. But none of them ever argued with Fernández about his and his friends' plans. When a man thinks he's going to bring freedom to his country, how can you tell him, "Don't bother, we're doing O.K. where we are now."

I wasn't going to say nothing too but Fernández, who was on his third Felipe Segundo and always got angry when he lost at gin, even just a couple of dollars, looked at me and said, "You think, Wolf, that we will not go through with our plans?"

"I didn't say nothing like that," I told him.

"Yes, but there is a certain look on your face that seems to doubt what I have just said."

"Don't worry about the look on my face." I said. "It don't have nothing to do with you."

"I understand from my brother-in-law," Fernández said, nodding at Slatsky, "that as a young man you were highly sympathetic to the Republicans in the Spanish Civil War. I believe you even went to Spain in one of those brigades fighting against Franco."

"Yeah," I said. "So?"

"You think, perhaps, the cause in Spain was more just than ours in Cuba? Even though they, and you, were on the same side with the communists? The same communists who then and now wish to destroy Mother Church, to remove from parents their children, to take away our property and our businesses. To control everything, from our thoughts to our actions."

Again, I didn't say nothing. I just stared at him. I felt my face getting hot.

I was just over twenty, at the University in Lublin, studying to become an engineer, which I never became. Me and my best friend Andrzej—we went through school together, we read the same books, we were like brothers—we volunteered for an International Brigade to fight for the Republic of Spain. Do you know about the Dabrowsky Brigade, which was mostly made up of Polish volunteers? And the Neftali Botwin Company, which was part of Dabrowsky, and composed of all-Jewish fighters? Look it up.

Lots of the volunteers were communists. But not all of us. Some of us were just anti-fascist. Me and Andrzej knew about Hitler. We knew about Mussolini. We didn't go there *for* Communism, but *against* Fascism, which was pure evil. The company got pretty much slaughtered. Andrzej was blown up as we were crossing the Ebro. Some, including me . . . survived.

Even when we were almost all wiped out, we sang and we shouted: "¡No Pasaran!"

They did.

And we lost.

I survived.

"So, do you still believe in the cause of those people?" Fernández demanded to know. "Do you oppose our trying to liberate our country from vermin like that? Whose side are you on anyway, Wolf?" He put on a little smile that looked like a tight mask across the lower part of his face.

"Look," I told him, "I ain't on nobody's side. I ain't against you and your friends invading no place. But I am against one thing. And that's your bullshit. The same bullshit week after week. I'm fed up with it and I don't want to hear no more of it!"

Fernández's face got hard and red. Everyone else was looking into their coffee cups.

"Le's go, Papi," Carmen said." She looked uncomfortable, but I don't think it was just from the argument I was having with Fernández. She had little pimples of sweat on her forehead.

Fernández finished off another glass of brandy "Yes, perhaps we should call it a night," he said. "Some of us must work tomorrow early," he said. Then he looked straight at Carmen and said: "And some of us undoubtedly must work tonight and the early hours of tomorrow."

"That's right, baby," Carmen said, "I gonna work the same side of the street tonight where is your mother."

Fernández stood and said very politely to Olga, "Thank you for the dinner." He turned to his wife, *"Vamanos."*

He and his wife started toward the door and I got up and stood in front of him. I came up to his long-pointed nose. "Who you talking to like that?" I said. "I wanna hear you apologize to her. Right now!" I felt my scalp tingling.

Fernández looked down at me. His mud-colored eyes were bloodshot. I saw hate boiling there, but also a tired irritation. He took a deep breath.

"That *puta* has insulted my sainted mother. I should be the one demanding an apology from that whore."

My arm went back to throw a punch. But Slatsky was there to catch it.

"Wolf, what's the matter with you?" Slatsky said. "Don't act crazy, please!" His light blue eyes had a deep pleading in them like I was about to upset more than just an evening for him.

I tried to pull my hand away, but Carmen jumped up and took a hold of my arm too. "Papi, Papi," she said.

Fernández grabbed his wife by the arm and yanked her to the door. She gave him a funny look. He opened the door and said to me, "You should be ashamed of yourself. An old man acting like that because of a young whore." He pulled his wife through the door and slammed it shut.

I was breathing heavy and I felt my heart pumping against my chest. Carmen went to the bathroom. Slatsky and Olga and me stood around without talking. Carmen came out and I mumbled something and we left.

We took a taxi back to the apartment. Carmen's little face looked pinched. It was twitching on the right side. I asked her what was the matter and she gave me a nervous smile and said, "Nuttin', baby. Don' worry. I gonna be O.K."

By the time we got back to the apartment Carmen looked terrible. She didn't have no color in her face, it was shiny with sweat.

"Papi," she said, "I need the dope, you know? I got to go and get some."

"I thought you wasn't going to take no more," I said.

"I know, I gonna quit tomorrow. But jus' tonight, I need some, you know?"·

I looked at her.

"I got to go out," she said. "I be back soon."

"How much money you need?" I said.

"Forty dollar," she said.

I gave her two twenties.

"*Gracias, mi amor.*"

She left and I got undressed and got into bed. At first, I thought: O.K., good, who needs the kind of trouble she can cause me? If I'm lucky, she won't come back.

I couldn't fall asleep. I got up and made myself a cup of tea and played a Mozart record. I got back into bed and lay there staring at the water-stained ceiling.

That sonovabitch Fernández, he put me back to Spain, to Extremadura, hotter than ovens and no water to drink, the German and Italian planes like locusts all over the sky, bombing and machine-gunning while we were in holes in the ground, to the Ebro, crossing the river, then having to hurry back; then back to Poland, then . . . which I don't go into in print. Then, after the war, wearing Russian Army pants and boots, a French Army shirt, an American Army sweater and jacket, on my back a German Army knapsack, going from Poland, across Germany, then through France, Belgium, Holland. Finally, the Jewish relief agency sends me to England, where I stay a couple of years, then the agency sends me to New York.

O.K., here's the beginning of my autobiography:

I was born, June 25, 1918, in the city of Vilnius, or Vilna, which at the time was claimed to be part of both Poland and Lithuania, then later became known as "the Jerusalem of Lithuania." I was born in a city that supposedly was founded because of a dream about—guess what? About a wolf!

Do you know about the Jews of Vilna? They were famous, among all the Jews in the world, and others, for their learning. The Gaon Elijah, who was the sage of the city back in the 18th Century, stood up for study and the intellect against the Hasidim when they started overdoing it with the cartwheels. And the courtyard of the Great Synagogue was surrounded by all sorts of houses of study, as well as prayer, going back to the 15th Century, and all the city's rabbis and scholars and poets and philosophers and politicians and merchants, and even in 1812 Napoleon walked and talked and mediated there.

And did you know that Lithuania became the largest state in all Europe in the 15th Century? That it became part of the Polish-Lithuanian Commonwealth before the Russians took it over, and that it became independent in 1918, just a year after I was born, before the Soviets and the Nazis moved in and wiped out people and the government's independence? We all got our history, filled with ups, downs and real evil and once in a while justice.

What I remember most about Vilna was something that happened when I was three, maybe four, years old. There was a typhoid epidemic there and my parents kept me and my two brothers in the house. It seemed like I was in there forever. My older brothers knew what was going on. But I was too young. I only knew that no matter what my parents said, I had to get outside to play. So I snuck out.

We lived in the last house on a long curving street that ran into the center of the city. Behind our house was woods and behind the woods was a road leading out of the city. My brothers and me and our friends grew up in those woods. We played there for years and knew every spot. The Potato Place, the clearing where we used to build fires and roast potatoes, some of my friends were later buried in a mass grave there.

I remember walking down the long street, past the houses. They were two-story homes like ours. I went past the little gardens and the shops, past my father's jewelry store, past what seemed like little boats lined up outside the houses. I wondered why there were boats in the street when the only ones I ever seen before were on the river.

My father came running after me. His face was white and he grabbed me hard on the arm and began pulling me back to the house. I asked him why the boats were outside the houses and not on the river. What boats, he yelled at me, what boats? I pointed to them. At first he didn't say nothing, he just stopped in the middle of the street and looked at me. Then he said they were a special kind of boat. People were sleeping inside them. I said I wanted a boat and started to cry. I can still see the way my father's eyes looked, tired and sad and frightened too.

When "sleep" came for my father and mother and three brothers and for my wife Sarah and for my precious Rachel, there wasn't boats for them to lie in. All there was was the air to carry the ashes and the smoke up into the sky.

And do you know about the rest of it? As far as the Jews in Vilna were concerned? That the Nazis penned them into the ghetto, then killed them all there? Except for some, who got out like my family, we went to Poland, years before. My father moved us to Lublin, where he went to work in the family's jewelry business. We left Vilna before the round-up. But it really didn't matter for my family—except for me. I won't go into that right now.

But now, in my head, I'm in London, at Hyde Park Corner. I'm listening to that big African guy, he's way over six feet, tribal scars all over his face, and he's black like you don't see in America. He's up there on a platform, shaking his fist at the faces looking up, telling them in a high-class English accent how if they don't free his people, they was all going to get their throats cuts "from ear to bloody ear." They shout back at him, but he don't pay no attention. Guys in peaked caps and with sandwich boards over them walk through the crowd handing out leaflets. They're advertising the end of the world. A little skinny guy with a Cockney accent is demanding that all the Jews in the crowd smuggle themselves into Palestine right away. Up on the platform there were also communists, socialists, anarchists, Gandhi followers, Arab nationalists, one-worlders, all sorts of what would now be called Jesus freaks.

I was working as a dishwasher in a restaurant in the Soho part of the city. Most of the time when I got a day off I went to Hyde Park Corner. The "entertainment" was free and the place fascinated me. All those different people shouting out what was going to save the world this time around. I remember when I was a kid that my father was a member of the Jewish Workers Bund, which was called *Allgemeiner Juedischer Arbeiter Bund in Polen, Russland und Lithuania.* He used to write articles in Yiddish, which was the Bund's language, for the newspaper where we lived. He believed with all his heart and soul in the Bund, that Russian socialism was the answer to the problems of the world, including the problems of the workers and problems of the Jews. The Bund was even against the Zionists. That was the atmosphere I was brought up in.

That was the "answer" then. After the Holocaust, for the Jews. Zionism became the "answer." I almost went along with it, almost tried to go to Palestine, which is now Israel. But something stopped me. I think it had something to do with those days at Hyde Park Corner. *Everyone* had problems—Jews, Arabs, Indians, Hindus, Muslims, Africans, the Irish, the displaced person, the working man, the one-worlders, the end-of-the-worlders, even the animal lovers who didn't want you to eat meat. And they *all* had the answer. Only, the Arab's answer was different from the Jew's answer, the one-worlder's was different from the end-of-the-worlders, and so on.

I know you got to, as they say, "separate the wheat from the chaff," which I always try to do. I know that some problems, and some answers, got to be taken more serious than others. I know my people have gone through hell over and over. And I also know only a great people could rise out of those flames again and again. And Zionism seemed the way to do it then.

But I decided not to go to Palestine. I had had enough of the Old World. I wanted to try to come up again in the New World. The "second time around," I wanted a new view on the human race, and on myself because just then I didn't think them or me was worth much.

When I woke again in the middle of the night, I thought: I want Carmen to come back. I would take her out to Boquerón, a little fishing village on the other side of the island. Julia, the woman who cleans my apartment once a week, owns a cabin there. It was her father's when he was alive, he was a fisherman. It ain't nothing but a shack, but I rented it from her before, for a couple of weeks. I would take Carmen there and give her one more chance.

I got up and made myself more tea. I went into the living room and sat in my old leather chair with the stuffing coming out of the arms and started reading a book about Mexico and the conquistadors. I couldn't concentrate.

Then Carmen came back. I gave her a key earlier. She opened the door and when she seen me sitting in the chair, she gave me a soft, sleepy smile. She came over and sat on the floor in front of me, then put her hand on my knee. I bent over and lifted her up and carried her into bed.

SIX

"Major studies on Puerto Rican migration, especially those written by North American scholars in the 1950s and 1960s, were focused on problem-oriented or blaming-the-victim cultural-deficit models commonly found in studies of poverty among U.S. minorities. These studies tended to recycle some common stereotypes and misconceptions about the disadvantaged conditions of Puerto Rican migrants."

A series of coughs from the instructor. He takes a handkerchief from his back pocket, blows his nose, excuses himself.

"The emergence of Puerto Rican Studies as a field of academic inquiry in the late 1970s fostered new historical and socioeconomic analyses of Puerto Rican migration and the formation of a US diaspora. It also generated a sustained critique of the shortcomings of previous scholarship and addressed the connections between US colonial domination in Puerto Rico and the structural and political factors that propelled island Puerto Ricans to migrate to the United States . . ."

Stevie, in an aisle seat in the last occupied row of the small, less than half filled auditorium, reads to himself what he wrote last night:

> At a little after his sixteenth birthday, Fico Ramírez went to sea, as a cabin boy on the British freighter Barry. That was where he learned an early lesson that both pained him and, in a way, set him free. What he learned was that the world is random, and yet our fates are fixed.

". . . New migration studies also began to document the history of Puerto Rican settlement and formation of stateside communities and to draw attention to migrants' productive lives and contributions to US society" reads the instructor of the University's newly created Department of the Puerto Rican Diaspora. "This new historiography includes several notable works, such as *Centro History Task Force 1979* that introduces a detailed account of the historical development of New York City's Puerto Rican community . . ."

> Fico's father, who was born in Corsica, met Fico's mother in San Juan, and they moved to the mountain town of Yauco to start a coffee plantation. Fico, whose full name was Francisco Miguel Antosanti Ramírez, was born in the mountains where he spent his first fifteen and a half years, going to school and helping out during the coffee harvest, when even his father was in the fields, directing the jíbaros picking the beans. All up and down the mountains, the men and women, in big straw hats and bandanas, stripped the plants, putting the ripe cherries into baskets hanging from their necks. Fico helped with the picking. It was really hard, really sweaty work, lots of times under a blazing sun, but it gave him a good feeling inside because he was part of something that happened every year with his help.

"*Torres and Velázquez 1978* . . . different forms of social and political engagement during the years of the civil rights movement . . . the contemporary transnational dynamics of a Puerto Rican nation moving between the island and the many U.S. states . . ."

> But sadness also entered Fico's life in the mountains. His mother died last year after she had her fifth son—she also had three daughters—and his father spent most of the time since then drinking and beating Fico and older brother Tato regularly. So they took off. Fico lived down by the docks for almost a year, on his own, except for the rats that he shared an old deserted warehouse with at night. During the day, he washed dishes at a restaurant on Fortaleza Street and delivered medicine to people from the drugstore down the street. He spent a lot of his free time walking around the waterfront, looking out to the bay and the ocean, wondering about his future life.
>
> When Fico heard that his father was looking for him to take him back to work on the farm, he got the cabin boy job on the Barry, which was docked in San Juan. The original cabin boy had gotten sick and was left in Jamaica. Fico spoke English well enough to get the job. In Yauco, his teachers were Americans . . .

He was finally able to start the novel last night. Up all night. Then work, lessons from Carlos. A snack at the hot dog stand by the harbor, then a bus to the University. He hears the prof's words, but can't really concentrate on them. He has to reread his own wonderful words.

> He helped serve the meals and washed the dishes and pots and pans and scrubbed down the mess room. He made the beds of the officers and cleaned their rooms. He scrubbed the heads. He ran across the deck delivering messages from the captain to the officers and served tea in the afternoons and got up at six in the morning and made tea for whoever was awake and at six-thirty he woke the rest of the crew. At night, he brought the food and other things for the next day's meals from the storeroom to the galley. He . . .

The bell rings. He'll skip the Teaching English as a Second Language class. He wants to get home and work on the rest of Chapter One. He crosses the campus down the path between the very tall, very slender, royal palms, (nothing like those in the Bronx), comes out the gate, goes to the bus stop for the Number One back to the Old City.

Before going to his apartment Stevie picks up a couple of *rellanos de papa* and a container of *mavi* at a *fritura* stand in the plaza. His dinner. Comparable to a couple of potato knishes and a Pepsi at Max's deli down the corner in the Bronx.

Up the hill to the highest street in the Old City, to the yellow paint-peeling four-story building. Up the creaky wooden stairs to the top floor. First on the left of the three apartments carved out there. He keys open the half tin-plated front door, moves across the living room-bedroom-kitchen (bathroom off the kitchen) to open the wooden doors (two of the louvers missing) to a tiny balcony from which, when you look afar, does not give the tenement view of overflowing garbage cans and scurrying rats in the South Bronx backyards of Stevie's growing-up years; instead, a panorama of ocean, sky, stars. Sun in the morning, moon at night. Closer up was La Perla, its crooked-roofed shacks slouching between the Old City's ancient walls and the now moon-sparked sea. Stevie steps out on the balcony where he has managed to squeeze in one typewriter-fitting table and two folded up metal chairs and squints at the watery moonlit path. He is ready to go to sea again.

Thanks to Mr. Wolf, who gave him those Conrad books, *Lord Jim, Nostromo, Chance.* Thanks to Mr. Conrad.

Look, here's the thing, here's where I'm at, after where I was. Soon after they were married, and had me—Esteban Juan

Díaz Calderón—my Mom and Dad, and of course me (I was six-months-old), we left Puerto Rico. That was 1959 and during those first years they were working in factories in New Jersey—sewing clothes, bottling drinks, baking Wonder Bread. The jobs were O.K. for Miguel "Mike" Díaz, who lost his last job on the island when the coffee plantation he was foreman at shut down, the owner selling the land so a shoe factory could come down from New York. The work was far from O.K. for Mom, who had a teacher's degree from the University of Puerto Rico, and found that "immigrants" were last to be hired in the New Jersey public schools. It wasn't until the move to the Bronx, among the thousands of other Puerto Rican refugees, that Mom, who wanted to bring the words and wisdom of Cervantes, Calderon de la Barca, García Lorca, et al to high school kids, was hired—as a kindergarten teacher.

What Stevie remembers about Jersey was the short time spent in Hoboken. The Elysian Fields, where the New York Knickerbockers played the first real baseball game ever, and, on other diamonds, where he played center field for the Hoboken Growlies in the Little League.

Just before the move to the Bronx, at his age of 13, God died in Puerto Rico. It happened when the plane in which Roberto Clemente was in to make sure the aid packages bound for the hurricane victims in Nicaragua got to them instead of being robbed by the goddamn frigging government officials who had robbed the goods on three earlier flights, when the overloaded plane went down after just taking off from the island, and Stevie felt he went down with his God. (He resurrected in Morris High, playing a fairly good right field on the varsity, before realizing in his late teens that he had career-ending trouble hitting curves, sliders, cutters.)

About Mike Díaz: a few more jobs in Bronx factories, and even one as a janitor in the school where Mom was teaching. Mucho rum, scotch, rye, bourbon; Papi's life like his drinks, on the rocks. Yet, believe it or not, not a bad Dad. At least Stevie and sister Millie were never mistreated by him, nor was Mom. Dad got drunk, came home once in a while, patted the kids on the head, took a "short nap" that lasted days, then disappeared again. After Stevie's ninth birthday, the young-old guy took the never-ending nap.

The wake: Papi lying there in the wooden box on a stand under the reproduction of a painting by the Puerto Rican artist, Tufiño of an old woman with a strong, hard-knock face wearing a red bandana. Below the picture and above the coffin, small crossed flags of Puerto Rico and the U.S. (the Stars and Stripes for Pfc. Pérez's two years in the Army, including frost-bite months at the frozen Chosin in Korea). Friends, neighbors, relatives coming through, taking quick glances at the skinny guy with the small smile just beneath the hairpin mustache on the seemingly rosy but sunken-cheeked face, head propped on the silky pillow, crossing themselves and mumbling something, then going into the kitchen for drinks of rum and small snacks and sweets.

Papi. I hardly knew ya'. Should I have tried harder to be your boy'? Should I have asked you to read to me, to sing Millie and me to sleep, to take me to ball games, to help me with my homework, Did I help drive you to drink? Of course not!

Mom, now head of the Spanish Department at Evander Childs High School, pissed when Stevie decided to return to Puerto Rico. He promised, he swore he would enroll at the University and get a degree. His high school grades weren't that bad and he was able to take night courses.

Why Puerto Rico, after almost 20 years in New York? Because he was . . . curious about the place where he was born . . . frustrated about his chances of getting *any*where in *La Gran Manzana* (non-college-degree jobs as a stock clerk, delivery "boy") . . . deeply saddened by the break-up with Sonia, who was sweet and lovely, and wanted marriage and babies, which he wasn't ready for, which made him feel guilty as hell because she was so sweet and—fuck it! . . . actually started to read good books (Hemingway, Steinbeck, et al) . . . wanted new experiences, adventures, most recently the Conrad books spurring him on—in his head, at least—to go to sea, and to write about it. Crazy as hell, but that's what he wanted more than anything—to write about his adventures as a cabin boy 50-60 years ago. In his head—from the Bronx to Borneo.

Something was nagging at him. A "yearning," which sounded too literary; it was something more . . . well, more *irritating*—in his head and in his heart. First, he was going to write that novel, then take off further on his own, in body, head, heart, soul. How's that for . . . whatthefuckever?

He sits at the table on the balcony, takes the *papa rellanas* from the greasy bag and washes them down with the *mavi*. Then he switches on the naked bulb over the balcony table, goes inside to the shelf on top of the closet, takes down his Olivetti 22, unzips the case, brings the typewriter out to the balcony, and goes back to Chapter One of his masterpiece.

SEVEN

I woke about eight o'clock and made coffee. Carmen was still sleeping; her mouth open catching flies and making rattling noises. I sat out on the balcony and drank the coffee. Then I went to my store.

When Don Alfonso came in, I told him I had to go to the states for a week on an emergency. I gave him the keys and asked if he would take charge while I was gone. He said, "of course" and told me not to worry.

Next, I went to see Julia. She lives in a small green wooden house in Barrio Obrero, a working-class section of Santurce. I took a bus there. I asked her about the house in Boquerón and she said she'd be glad to let me use it. At first, she said she didn't want no money, but I made her take a check for a hundred fifty dollars.

When I got back to the apartment, Carmen was still sleeping. I shook her awake.

"We're gonna go for a trip to the country."

Her little face broke into a smile. "That's the truth, Papi?"

"Yeah," I said. "Come on."

She jumped out of bed like a young kid. I made us omelets and while we were eating I told her where we were going—and why.

"O.K.," she said. "I gonna do whatever you say."

We went to La Perla to get her clothes. People and wash were hanging over the balconies of the houses bunched together on the top of a steep hill that led down to the ocean. Radios were blaring, kids were running around yelling, dogs were barking and searching for food from overflowing garbage cans. Between the houses, you could see the ocean winking a huge blue eye. Jukeboxes were blasting away from the poolrooms and bars along the main street and young guys were standing on the corners and in the doorways, drinking beer, smoking cigarettes and other things and looking at us with small smiles on their tough faces. We started down some broken concrete steps and went through alleyways so narrow you had to almost go sideways. Naked kids were sitting in dirty puddles splashing each other and old men were snoozing on hammocks on porches while roosters and chickens were strutting and fluttering in back yards. I ain't been to La Perla for years, but nothing changes there.

Further down, the houses were small shacks with no porches. I could see inside the small square windows to the Christs on the walls and people moving around and there was a heavy sweet and rancid smell, it's the smell of very poor people everywhere. We kept going down steps until we got to the beach, where beer cans, broken bottles, splintered wood, crushed cardboard, old mattresses, and rusty bed springs were lying around. A gang of kids and skinny dogs were running across the beach and into the water there. There was even a pig going through the trash.

"That's my house over there," Carmen said. It was on stilts by the water and bleached white from the sun and salt spray. The ocean, which looked calm far out, was rumbling and foaming and crashing against rocks below the house. The hot salty smell in the air mixed with a sewer smell and stung inside your nose.

We went inside. A young girl with black hair to her waist sat on a wooden box watching TV in a dark, dank room. She was wearing a white tee shirt and jeans. She was a beautiful kid. Flickering across the screen was a cartoon of a big guy with a bat chasing a little guy like a scary dream a young kid might have. The sea rumbled under the floor.

Carmen greeted her sister and she turned light green eyes from the TV to her. They were empty, those eyes.

"You eat breakfast?" she asked the kid in Spanish. The kid nodded.

"Rafi home?"

The kid shook her head. I was glad. I wasn't feeling like meeting Carmen's brother.

"This is Mr. Wolf," Carmen said to her sister. "This is my sister Millie."

The kid's empty eyes looked through me. Her mouth hung open slightly.

"She's . . . you know like a little retarded." Carmen said. Then she told me to come to her room. We went behind a red curtain behind the TV. The "room" was small. It was separated by another red curtain from an area behind it. It didn't look like part of the house I was in. It didn't look like part of any house I ever seen.

The walls were painted a glowing orange, the ceiling was purple and pasted up there was hundreds of little gold stars like they give out at school and a cut-out silver moon with a face on it. The face had cat's green eyes and whiskers and a turned-down mouth. The few pieces of furniture were painted bright red and green and yellow. Carmen's clothes, just as bright colored, were hanging on an open rack. Set out in perfect order on the floor under the clothes were dozens of pairs of shoes. All over the walls were rows and rows of snapshots. Carmen was in all of them—with soldiers, sailors, cops, priests, waiters, postmen, firemen, some guy in a turban and long robe and beard down to his chest, boyfriends, girlfriends, babies, old folks, kids, dogs, cats, cows, pigs, horses, rabbits, parrots and there was one with a monkey on her shoulder and another with a big snake curled around her arm and she was smiling into the camera. The pictures were taken in bars, in homes, on the beach, in the countryside, on roofs of buildings, in cars, in the streets of San Juan and New York. Some were faded and crinkled and peeling with brown spots on them. Those were the ones of her when she was a little kid, a cute little thing in pigtails, with already something shrewd in her eyes. On one wall, above the photographs, there was a painting of the Crucifixion. Christ looked handsome and girlish and his eyes were almost up in his head.

Carmen saw me looking at the picture. "Maybe I take that, huh Papi?"

"Let it stay," I said. "You can get it later."

"He always wit' you in your heart if you wanna keep Him there, right?"

"Yeah."

"He took all our sins wit' him up there on the cross, right?"

I grunted. "Let's get going," I said.

From under the bed, Carmen pulled out an old beat-up suitcase, a big cardboard thing with metal on the edges, and started folding her dresses into it. There wasn't enough room in there for the clothes she was taking back to the apartment and to the country, let alone her shoes. She went behind the other curtain and came back with three or four shopping bags. I put her shoes in the bags and she tucked some clothes down the sides.

When we were ready to go, Carmen said, *"Ay, bendito,* I don' want to leave Millie here wit'out me. I don't trust my brudder to take care of her. Do you mind if I take her to my aunt's house, she lives up in the mountains? It's on the way to where we're going."

"How far in the mountains?"

"Not far."

What the hell? "Yeah, O.K.," I said.

So Carmen got out some more shopping bags and we packed Millie's things too. Millie started crying, she didn't want to leave the TV. Carmen told her they had one where she was going.

We got back to my apartment and Carmen called her aunt to say she was bringing Millie. She put what she wanted for the week into her suitcase and left the rest in the shopping bags and I packed too. Then we took a taxi to Río Piedras where we got a publico to Barranquitas, the town where Carmen's aunt lived.

We climbed up narrow winding mountain roads. We passed concrete houses and wooden shacks right on the edge of the road or hanging on the sides of the dark green hills. The countryside was thick with trees and bushes and plants and flowers. It smelled wonderful. It was a relief to get out of San Juan for a change.

From high up on a mountain road, we could see spotted cows lying in the grass below. They looked like little toys. Carmen pointed them out to her sister and for the first time since we started out the kid smiled, and she reached her hand out the window like she was grasping for one of the toy cows down below.

We passed under fire red umbrellas which were flamboyant trees and then we went by some banana trees with bananas hanging in thick bunches like fat green fingers under the large drooping leaves.

The publico drove up to Carmen's aunt's house and honked its horn. Carmen's aunt came out on the porch. The house wasn't no wooden shack. It was big, pink and concrete and surrounded by green hills, and further off by high mountains you could see from the terrace in the back. There was a big station wagon parked in front of the house.

Carmen's aunt was wearing a white blouse, checkered slacks, and tennis shoes. She had curly red hair, a couple of chins, a big mole on her cheek, little amber-colored eyes and a wide mouth that with a smile took up half her face.

A big brown and white mutt came running down the steps of the house wagging its bushy tail. It jumped up on Carmen's sister and she petted and hugged it and let it lick her face.

"*Hola, Pepe, como estás?*" Carmen's sister kept saying over and over like she was real concerned. The dog started to bark and Carmen's sister pulled away and looked like she was going to cry, and Carmen's aunt whacked the dog on the behind and told the girl: "Don't cha worry, *quierida*. He's just saying, 'I'm so glad to see ya—where you been so long?' We're both so glad to see ya."

Carmen introduced me to her aunt, Rosa, who opened half her face in another smile. There was gold teeth in different parts of her mouth.

"She just stay for a couple of days this time," Carmen said. "It's O.K.?"

"*Como no,*" Rosa said. "Sure t'ing. Come on." She took the bags from me and put them in the house and then we went out to the terrace in the back.

Rosa wasn't no simple country woman. She had a bar out back there and she was drinking Chivas Regal scotch. I had a rum and Coke and Carmen and her sister had Cokes. Rosa was about sixty years old. She kept calling me "boy."

"Hey, boy, you wan anudder drink?" and "Listen, boy, I lived forry-five years in New York. I worked all the time at Ben Mor dress factory, in the garment center, on Forry-Firs' Street and Sevens Avenue, you know, boy? I was shop steward there. International Ladies Garment Workers, Local twenty-two, I'm stickin' with the union, you know what I mean, boy?" Then the mouth would open like a cavern and a huge cackling laugh would roll out and skip across the countryside.

Rosa was a non-stop talking machine. One of those persons, once they start talking, something builds up inside them and takes over and keeps going full speed ahead and when it meets something in its path like words from someone else, it gets louder and stronger and rolls right over the other words.

"I left here when I was fifteen," Rosa said. "I buy this house with the money I saved from workin' at the dress factory. So now I am retired and living like a queen, you know, boy?

"I been through four husbands, eight kids, sixteen gran'children and at different times I supported them all. O.K., three husbands, I won't count Fede, that *sinvergüenza*. So now I gonna take it easy, you know? I ain't gonna do just nothin'. I have parties here all the time. But I ain't workin' no more, I'm gonna enjoy myself, you know? We Puerto Ricans know how to have a good time. You got to come back to my house for a party next weekend, O.K.?

"Lemme tell you somet'ing, boy. When I left the island, people was starvin' here. It was a pity, kids running around with swelled up bellies and arms and legs like toothpicks. That's why I left for New York. No work here. And I didn't go on welfare, neither. Not me! As soon as I got there, I got a job at the Ben Mor dress factory. Forty-First Street and Seventh Avenue (this time she made sure to pronounce the t's). Ben and Morris Seltzer, they was brothers. They both died five years ago. From heart, you know? They died two weeks from each other.

"I didn't have no easy life, boy. Not like today. A lot of people still ain't got jobs, but they all got food stamps so everybody eatin'. I don't grudge them though. At least kids ain't starvin' no more with puffed up bellies. But the food stamps keep the adults from looking for work. All they do is sit and watch the television.

"There's lots of prejudice in New York against the Puerto Ricans. But let me tell you somet'ing. Nobody looked down on me! Because I told them I was as good as any of them, and I showed it too. But you got to say it. You keep telling them over and over and they get the idea. I stick up for me, and for my people, and for the workers. So that's why they make me shop steward."

"New York is my favorite place, but deep down I am a Puerto Rican. So that's why I come back here. I feel in my home in both places, you know what I mean? I don' let nobody push me around no place. Everyone, they love me. Except my enemies. I got plenty of them, too. I tell people what I think, they don' like that." She started cackling again like it was the funniest thing in the world that people don't like it when you tell them what you think.

"The people here, they don't tell you to your face how they feel," Rosa said, shaking her head like she didn't understand that. "And they accept whatever happen to them. They say it's fate, there's nuttin' they could do." She kept shaking her head. "Listen, boy," she said, "I don't go to church no more, but I still religious in my heart, you know? But I don' think that way, that there's nuttin' you could do because it's God's will. Sometimes you got to let God know when He pissin' you off, you know?"

Rosa went on for another hour. But I didn't care. I enjoyed sitting out on her terrace and drinking her rum, half-listening to her and looking out at the green hills and the trees and smelling the hot, sweet country air. The smell reminded me of summer vacations when I was a kid. It brought back childhood. And then I got a deep, sad feeling. I said we better be going. Rosa took us in her station wagon to the town plaza where we got another publico.

By the time we got to Boquerón, it was already dark and Carmen was fidgety and nervous. The shack was on a dirt road near the public beach. From the back window, you could see out across Boquerón Bay, it was still and black, except for a couple of lights from boats way out on the water. The sky looked like it had a million pin-pricks in it with light shining through the tiny holes.

It was calm outside, but Carmen wasn't so calm inside the house. She walked back and forth and tried to smile, but she couldn't. Her face was damp and gray, it looked like a dirty rag.

"I don' feel good," she said. "I got to vomit." She staggered off to the bathroom which was outside in the back of the house. I heard her puking her guts up. When she came back, she didn't look no better. Her eyes were teary and her nose was running. She crumbled on a couch.

"I feel so weak like my bones is melting. Everything hurt. Like I gonna die." She was crying. She started twisting from side to side and making low moaning sounds. Parts of her body began twitching. Then she started shivering.

I took a sheet from my suitcase and put it over her. Her teeth were chattering, but she was sweating too. She kept turning and twisting and twitching and moaning.

"I feel so bad. I don't got no strength and everything hurt inside me. I need some dope, you know."

"You can't get none out here," I told her. "You just got to hold off. I'm gonna be here with you."

Carmen didn't say nothing. She turned on her stomach, got up on her knees, arched her back and put her head under her chest. Then she collapsed back on her stomach. She turned on her back, stretched her legs out, pulled them up toward her stomach and put her arms around her knees and pushed her head back. It hung off the couch. She was panting and gasping like something was stuck in her throat. Then she turned to the side and said, "I got to go to the bathroom." She put one foot on the floor, then started falling off the couch. I caught her. She vomited some green stuff on me.

It went on like this for hours. Her little face seemed to get smaller and smaller like it was about to collapse in on itself. She kept squeezing her features together like she was trying to find a place to concentrate all the pain. Like she would feel better if she could bring all the pain to a point in her head, even if she had to collapse the bones and skin up there. She kept saying, "I wanna die, I wanna die."

I couldn't do nothing for her. Except cover her when she started shaking and wipe her face with a towel when she was sweating. And help her to the bathroom outside even when nothing was coming out of her. And sit beside her and sometimes hold her hand.

Finally, she wore herself out and fell into a half sleep. She was still moaning and twitching around, but it was more subdued. I sat in a chair near the couch. I fell asleep and I woke up and I fell asleep in that chair, I don't know how many times in the next three, four days.

It was hell, I ain't gonna describe it no more. Except to say I kept dreaming my bones was turning to jelly and the rest of me was melting into a pool of liquid, except for my eyes which were seeing everything. I was dreaming I was becoming the way Carmen said she felt.

It was hell.

EIGHT

Doris sang:

> "I don't know why but I'm feeling so sad
> "I long to try something I never had
> "Never had no kissin'
> "Oh, what I've been missin'

Soft, lovely, tinkling arpeggios on the piano by Paul Warren. He furrowed a long brow at the keys, then snuck a look up at Doris, who, unsure of her timbre—too dark? Too floozy-like?—smiled wanly at him. He smiled back, looked back down at the keys.

Doris sang: slowly, but in a steady, more definite rhythm, and with feeling:

> "The night is cold, and I'm so alone
> "I'd give my soul just to call you my own
> "Got a moon above me
> "But no one to love me
> "Lover man, oh, where can you be?"

Dale Jones, on his trombone, slid out notes —long, sad—then a little growl. Then long slides again.

Let him wail, Doris. He'll set up the last chorus, then I'll just get to the heart like Billie . . . hope against hope.

> "Someday we'll meet
> "And you'll dry all my tears
> "Then whisper sweet
> "Little things in my ear
> "Hugging and a-kissing
> "Oh, what I been missing
> "Lover man, ohhh, where can you be?"

She dug down and it came out. Nice. She felt it. Almost all the way. It came out . . . nice. The applause was . . . nice. Not overwhelming, but . . . appreciative. "¡Chévere!" shouted one guy standing in the back. "Groovy!" Not bad. Almost, almost.

Doris returned to the bar, from where she had been coaxed by Paul to sing—"Come on, sweetie, just one." So she did it, then downed her rum on the rocks and ordered another.

Paul came over to her after the set. "Nothing *you're* missing—voice-wise," he said. "You got those hanging phrases back. You got the wistfulness, just like Billie. You sound great!"

So the more she sounds like Billie, the less she sounds like Doris Jackson. So how great is that?"

A little rusty," she said. "Trouble with the lowest notes."

"You could work that out in a week. Come on back, sweetie. I miss you like mad." He blinked those spidery lashes. "We *all* miss you. You were, you are, well . . . you know . . . dumbass me."

A long, lovely index finger to his lips. "No, it wasn't you. It was me. It was *all* me."

"How long since you've been back here? Eight months, right?"

"Just a little over three months."

"It seems like years . . . centuries . . . eons!"

Doris smiled, warm and real. She missed this guy. She missed the whole funky scene. A jazz joint near the beach in San Juan. Locals—ex-pats and "natives" who loved the music, making it and digging it. Paul was no second-rate musician. He had recorded with Ben Webster; Roy Eldridge had even sat in one late night after appearing with Ella at the Americana Hotel in Isla Verde.

One night—what? A year ago?—she had got up the courage to ask him if she could try out her rusty voice on just one number.

"Of course," he said. "If your voice is as lovely as the rest of you, that should be terrific," he lied. She knew she was falling apart—head, body, heart, soul . . .

> "Ooh, ooh, ooh
> "What a little moonlight can do
> "Ooh, ooh, ooh
> "What a little moonlight can do to you . . ."

Not too shabby. Paul loved it. He invited her for a late-night snack. In his small, sort of shabby, but cozy apartment in a three-story building a couple of blocks from the beach. He scrambled up a couple of Westerns. They washed them down with cognac-laced coffee. He stacked his LPs—Ellington and Tatum and Billie, Sarah, Ella.

She allowed him free access to her forty-five-year-plus body. He was a few years younger, but, to her, seemed almost like a kid. Kissing, licking, then Wham! Bam! *I want you, sweetheart! I need you, sweetheart! Oh, Jesus, Mary, Whatthefuckever!*

She sang with the combo on the weekends, stayed with Paul those nights. Bessie was brought over, bitching, to his apartment. Late night dinners, licking and loving and going to the beach for Sunday swims before hotel brunches. He was kind, considerate, what the hell more could she want? She loved Paul—body, heart, soul, etc.

Then, for reasons that (or is it which?) no rational explanation could know of, she didn't love him. After all was not said and not done, she knew she did not deserve to love him. She quit singing and quit Paul on the weekends and returned, with a vengeance to rum and just made it mornings (missing many) to work at *El Pajaro de Oro*. Golden, she wasn't—not by a long ways.

But now, she would give it another go, return to the roots of what her being should be. Just the weekends.

Saturday night. Doris, dressed in basic black (was the skirt too short?), did three sets with the combo, rationed herself to two rums with plenty of Coke (like in Cola) and, after another after-midnight Western omelet at Paul's, had just a few after-dinner tokes from Paul's pipe. Between puffs, as they sat on the green-and-red flowery covered couch, they watched a very late show dubbed-into Spanish John Wayne movie (Paul said it was *The Searchers,* a classic; he explained the not-to-hard-to-follow kidnap and rescue plot.) Then he told her for the umpteenth time that night how terrific her singing was, then said: "Look, sweetheart, we got a good thing going—again. I probably did some dumbass things the last time."

No, baby, it was me. It was all me.

"So let's give it another go, O.K.? You still get your job in the Old City, right? And I still got the lessons and the classes at the Observatory. So I would like you to move in here, permanent, with me, we do our things during the day, and our music things at night, and we pool our money and we can live like, well like any other couple. You want to go to City Hall and get a certificate that's O.K. with me."

"We both aren't officially divorced," said Doris.

"Damn!" said Paul. "Damn! Damn!"

They both burst out laughing.

Then Paul said: "Love is more important than marriage. What d'ya say?"

"I'll see what Bessie says," Doris said.

One week, ten days of chicken-heartedness. Then Doris decided to stop being such a drag. On herself, among others. Well, she would give it a go. But again on the weekends, for starters. Take a few things over there.

While she was packing a small suitcase, carefully folding the one-and-only Versace, the "postbox-red stretch-jersey detailed with lilac cross-stitch embroidery and slashed at the hem for a signature hit of glamour" (she kept the description on the bill pinned to the dress, which she bought *very* wholesale on a recent trip to New York), Bessie decided the time was ripe to jump into the suitcase, lick her paws, then call out to complain about the move, or maybe, hopefully, to say "I'm ready to go."

Doris picked Bessie up, sat with her on both their favorite Dominican rocker, rocked her and tickled her throat and belly until Bessie squealed, "enough," and twisted off Doris' lap. She looked up from the straw mat, then twisted her head like she would never understand what Doris, and undoubtedly all humankind, was about. She padded off to her water bowl in the kitchen beyond.

Doris went back to the closet and was about to pull down Bessie's carrying case, then decided to do it in the morning. She didn't want to give Bessie the opportunity to start pitching a bitch, crying out "Not again!" when she saw her transportation unit being readied to cage her in one more time.

"Bessie, baby, it's just for the weekend. We'll give it a try again."

The phone call came at 3 a.m. by the alarm clock on the dresser. Maybe the fifth or sixth ring.

"What?"

"It's me, my darling. Calling to say I love you and I miss you."

Paul? No. I'm "sweetheart" to him. Not "darling."

Of course, even two-thirds asleep, she knew. She knew it wasn't Paul. Oh, Shit! Hang up, Doris! Hang the fuck up!"

"Long time, darling. Too long. I want to see you again. I'll be coming down to the island in a couple of days. Where are you living these days?"

"I . . . What? . . . No . . . I . . . How? . . ."

"Yeah, you're not listed. I got your number from the store where you're still working. I had Sylvia call, tell them there was a family emergency, and some nice guy got her your phone number. So where are you living? Still in Old San Juan?"

"I'm in the middle of moving."

"From where to where?"

Silence.

"Come on, baby, where will you be staying?

"No, I won't . . ."

"You know I'll find you. I always do. "Cause deep down you *know* you really want to see me."

Silence.

"See you soon, bitch!"

Both parties slammed down their phones.

NINE

It was hell, but we came out of it.

We spent ten days in Boquerón. Carmen was on her feet again after those four days. We went to the beach on the good days and bought little oysters from the vendors in the street and squeezed lemon on them and slipped them down our throats, they were sweet and delicious, and we ate fresh fish in restaurants and sat on the back porch of the house watching it get dark over the bay. The sky looked like the largest canvas ever, stretched to the sea, a blue purple painting with pink and orange and crimson slashes.

Carmen got a dark coppery color from the sun. She looked like an Indian. I got the color of the lobsters I ate for dinner. In the evenings I read the books I brought along. One book was about how the conquistadors destroyed the Indians in the Caribbean. It was by a Spanish friar, De las Casas. The other book was about the life of Leonardo da Vinci. I bought Carmen a small transistor radio and she spent most of the evenings listening to salsa music and painting her toenails. She made them all colors—gold, green, purple, black. Sometimes she just sat around thinking. I didn't ask her about what. I bought a sketch pad and did sketches of her on the beach and back at the cabin. One night she flipped through the book about Leonardo, looking and smiling at the pictures. Then she got interested in the other book, especially the part about the Spanish burning and roasting Indians and throwing them to the dogs. I drew her with her eyebrows bunched together and her forehead creased as she read, her finger going slow across the page.

"Them Spanish was mossafuckers," she said.

I grunted. "There was worse than them," I said.

"You mean where you was at?" Carmen said.

"How do you know about that?"

"I hear about it," Carmen said. "People said you was in one of them Nazi places, right? That's why you got the numbers on your arm, ain't it?"

"Yeah," I said.

"What they do to you there?"

"Nothin'," I said.

"Was they as bad to the Jews like the Spanish was to the Indians?"

"No," I said.

"No?" She sounded disappointed.

"What's the matter wit' you?" I said. I could feel my head getting light. "Don't you know nothin'?"

"I sorry, baby," Carmen said. "I ain't been too far in school."

I grunted. "Hold still, I got to draw you," I told her.

"O.K.," Carmen smiled. She held still. She was getting to be a good model.

The next night Carmen told me things about herself. Things that were like clichés for someone with her background, which didn't make them less horrible. How her father left when she was a baby. How one of her mother's boyfriends raped her when she was twelve. How she went to New York on her own when she was fifteen and met some guy and lived with him, he was a junky and made her one too and sent her out as a prostitute to get money for drugs for them. How the guy died one night from an overdose, she found him with his head in the toilet bowl. And how for the last thirteen years of her life she been selling her body and using the money to buy drugs. Except for six months, when she got a job in a shoe factory in New Jersey and stayed off drugs and even went to night school to learn English. And then another time for two months when she worked at Woolworth's on Fourteenth Street in New York. But except for those two times she's been going out night after night for almost half her life, in Brooklyn, the Bronx, El Barrio, and San Juan to find two, three guys a night to put their pricks inside her cunt so's she could get money for the heroin she needs inside her veins.

"I like to take the dope," she said. "But I tired going out and gettin' the money, you know? It's a real drag."

"Why you like to take drugs?" I was upset that she said she enjoyed it.

"'Cause it makes me relaxed, you know."

"But you don't need it now, right?"

"No, Papi, not now," Carmen said. "I know it ain't good for me and I ain't gonna take it no more. I finish wit' dat shit and the way I been livin'. I jus' need you to help me and I gonna be straight. I wanna make somethin' better in my life, you know?" Maybe you could give me more books about the Spanish mossafuckers and what they done to the Indians, 'cause I both, Spanish and Indian, right Papi? So I can read what one part of me done to the other part, you know?"

I grunted.

As soon as we got back to Old San Juan, we went to the overpriced, American-owned supermarket a few doors down from my store and bought lots of food, steaks and potatoes and fruits and fresh vegetables, to build Carmen up so she don't look like a toothpick no more.

I sent Carmen back to the apartment with a delivery boy, then went to my store. I had a surprise waiting for me. The police was there. The store was broken into the night before. They didn't get into the safe for the valuable stuff, but they smashed three showcases and took a lot of silver. They also stole Puerto Rican santos and Spanish swords and other things. About a dozen shelves were cleared off. They got in through the small window high up in the stockroom on the second floor, cutting through the grating up there. I'd have to seal up the window with cement.

Don Alfonso kept apologizing to me like it was his fault. I told him, don't worry about it, they didn't take nothing too valuable. I wasn't all that upset. I was even friendly with everyone the rest of the day. Being with Carmen was making me almost human.

When I got home Carmen cooked steaks and baked potatoes and we had them with wine and apple pie and coffee and then we went to the Italian ice cream place a couple of doors down on the plaza. We both had a big sundae which we took to the benches in the plaza and ate them and watched the people pass by and looked up at the moon. It was so clear you could see the mountains on it.

"You think anyone like us, is living up there?" Carmen asked me.

"Not on the moon."

"What about other places up there?" She waved her hand at the sky.

"Maybe," I said.

"You think they got it better there than we got it here?"

"If they're like us down here, they probably screwed up their place also."

"But maybe they learned," Carmen said. "There's always hope if you learn how to live a better life, right, Papi?

I grunted. Carmen smiled and nodded.

We went back upstairs and I put on the Mozart Symphony Number Forty-One and started on another painting of Carmen. She posed for me, but again, besides Carmen it looked like my first wife Sarah too.

After a couple of hours, we sat out on the balcony and one of the cruise ships down in the harbor let out a loud deep moan from its foghorn, it sounded like some giant sea monster grieving about something. Carmen jumped. I asked her if she would like to go on a cruise someday and she looked at me with wide eyes, then narrowed them—like I surprised her but then she suspected I was kidding, which I wasn't—and she said, "Sure."

We went inside and made love and we did it again in the morning before I went to the store and, in the next few days, in the nights, and it was like I was eighteen again. I'm surprised I didn't get a heart attack. But it was like some life force took over my body, it was asleep a long time. And Carmen said she was starting to feel again in her body too, which she ain't done for so many years because of the drugs.

At night we'd go for ice cream after dinner and sit in the plaza for about an hour and then I'd work on the painting, it was turning out different from anything I done before. When you first looked at it, Carmen-Sarah looked calm and peaceful like Sarah who was always at peace with herself, or the way Carmen looked when she was on drugs. But the more you looked in the eyes, the more you seen the terror deep inside there. Like Sarah when they took her away from me after we got out of the cattle car that brought us to Auschwitz. Or like Carmen, which is the thing deepest in her, it made her take drugs. The hair was hanging straight to her waist, it was black like Carmen's, but it had reddish streaks too because Sarah had red hair. The more I painted the portrait, the more uncomfortable I felt.

I seen what it was. The terror was deep in the eyes. But something else was there. I was being accused in those eyes. We were on the platform and they grabbed Sarah and my daughter, Rachel, she was seven years old, and dragged them away from me and there was nothing I could do. Nothing I did. I should of done something. I should of tore out the eyes of the pig that dragged them away. I should have done it and then got killed by the guns that were aimed at us when we got to the station. I should of done something.

But I didn't. I just heard my little Rachel whimpering and looked into my wife, Sarah's, eyes. And seen the terror there. And the accusing too. Which I may have put there later. But which is there now, forever.

Carmen was to me now like Sarah and Rachel then. I wasn't going to let her get dragged away by drugs. Heroin was different from the gas chamber. It took longer. It was a living death, which is maybe worse than just dying.

I wasn't going to let Carmen get dragged away.

I tried to bring good things into her life. I played her my Mozart records, which she listened to, even though I knew she'd rather be listening to salsa music. "You know why Mozart is so good?" I told her. "Because the music comes from the heart and the head at the same time. Everything you felt in your life, it's there in the music, except it's more happy than sad."

Carmen gave me a dreamy smile. "I know what you mean, Papi."

Maybe she did.

Once in a while we went to the movies. Carmen liked horror films and I sat through them. They bored me as much as they made her excited. She let out little cries and dug her fingers into my arm. I think she liked them because she could pretend she was a kid again. I took her to the casino a couple of times and she watched while I played blackjack.

I explained the game to her, but she didn't want to play.

"I don' wanna lose your money," she said.

I showed her my art books and she looked interested in the paintings. I told her we would go to the museums in New York where they got some of those paintings and we'd go to good restaurants and see shows and concerts and she looked at me like I was talking about a trip to Mars, but she said, "Yeah, I wanna go wit' you. I wanna see them t'ings."

I bought her books about the Spanish and the Indians and the Nazis and the Jews. She said she was reading the books while I was at work, I wasn't going to give her no quiz on them. She could never get from books what it was like anyway.

We was going good like this for a couple of weeks. Then things started to get screwed up again.

TEN

> The ship was being lifted into the air, and it was quivering like there was an earthquake in the ocean. Then it plunged down with a crashing roar and I was somehow holding on to . . . a mast? A spar? Ropes, cables, chains.
>
> The ship kept rising and shuddering over the giant waves, then crashing down, and my insides were tugging and twisting, but I stayed up there on the deck and then the giant face came through the gray-black sky and started booming down and I kept nodding like I was getting the message, whatever the hell it was, coming from whoever the hell?

Stevie was recording the dream in the small black notebook he kept on the table by his bed. Actually, the face and the voice coming through the heavens was not all that huge and booming. More questioning, even with a guilty look. More poor drunk Papi than God all-mighty. So why was he exaggerating it in his notebook? He'd make it more dramatic when it gets transcribed into . . .whatthefuckever. Now, write it like it was. A drunk Papi, wondering . . . What? Why he had to leave so early? No, that was Stevie's question. Papi was explaining, sort of. "You see, my son, it wasn't because of you. It was . . . what it was."

No, mea culpa, Papi! It *was* my fault. We, the sons, kill their fathers.

He wrote:

> "Am I sure that face wasn't the face of a guilty God? No. Sure I'm sure."

He looked at the travel alarm clock on the dresser. 6:30. Three hours before he had to go to work. He didn't want to go back to sleep.

He ate the leftover half of one of the potato *rellanas* from last night and washed it down with a Pepsi from the small fridge. He'd pick up a sandwich and coffee later and bring them to the store, where he would "breakfast" in the stockroom. He showered, dressed.

He wanted to go for a walk. To make sure, for some weird reason, that he was where he was: Puerto Rico, San Juan, the Old City.

Down the four flights, then along the Boulevard Del Valle, the highest street in the Old City. Spanish forts, now tourist walkabouts, on each end of the boulevard. Along the sidewalk, fronds on the skinny palms waving like messy hairdos. El Morro Fortress, fronted by a huge lawn once used by the U.S. military for parades, then a golf course, now a kite-flying green field for kids, moms, and pops. Along the street, sloping down passed the cemetery, the old Spanish walls, meant to keep out the Brits and the Dutch invaders. The upper walls, now a barrier between the pastel-colored colonial homes along the hilly streets and the La Perla slum shacks sloping down to the ocean. Above the shacks, against the still orangey early morning sky, crisscrossing antennas looking like paintings by that Dutch artist (that guy who paints the crisscrossing lines?— Mondrian!) Beyond La Perla—The Sea. (The *veiny* sea? Maybe.)

Off the boulevard, down the blue-cobbled streets, through the alleys—some of the post-midnight cats still out and around, licking curbside crevices. Past the ground-floor homes of the poor, looking into the always open windows, already the smell of garlic, peppers, onions, tomato sauce, along with strong coffee, coming through and mixing—*gracias a Dios*—with the streetside sewer smells. In a ground-floor apartment on Calle Sol, a girl mimics in perfect English the voice of Diana Ross singing "Stop, in the Name of Love."

The rum-soaked homeless are hunched over and the junkies are nodding as they sit along the low wall on Calle Tanca between Luna and San Francisco Streets. The old men already are there on the benches, figuring fortunes on horse-racing forms or just staring down the day.

The guy with the cardboard box over his head is out on the street, screaming under the box, then tearing it off and looking around frantic like he had to find who was driving him nuts yelling under there. He's a young guy, not more than thirty, with a slim, handsome face and long sideburns, he looks like a bullfighter. Poor guy.

Stevie picks an orange from the pile on a red-and-yellow cart and the street vendor peels it via an attached cranking machine and the skin comes off like twisted confetti. He gives the vendor a quarter, digs into the fruit as he heads down to the bay area. The onetime pets, now-escapee parakeets are chattering up a high-pitched storm in the trees opposite the U.S. post office (the projected scene of Carlos' Good Friday Uprising).

Stevie moves down to the post office. Will the old guy who runs the newspaper kiosk in front of the building be open for business on Good Friday to witness the takeover, the declaration of the Puerto Rican Republic?

The guy's on-the-scene comments, his blotted, blubbery face looking wide-eyed into the camera, behind him the kiosk stacked with newspapers, magazines, lottery tickets, sunglasses, candy bars—pictured in all the newspapaers and on TV, locally and around the states, even around trhe world, especially if it's a slow news day.

Stevie mounts the front steps to the three-story building, into the corridor, past the PO boxes, to the staircase to the second floor, where offices that do business for the towering federal court building behind are located. Balconied archways onto the street along the outside corridor. Waist-high metal grates by the archways, perfect places to hang one or more Puerto Rican flags when declaring the Republic. Stand behind there, lean over, shout down, possibly use a megaphone. (Logistics to be worked out on how to enter what on Good Friday should be a locked building, maybe a guard or two posted outside.)

Stevie moves to a balconied archway. He looks down over the street starting to come alive with gleaming vehicles and men sauntering by in work clothes and, occasionally, in suits. Soon, the government office-working curvy young women with long and straight and curly black and red and even blond hair will be swaying toward their offices, pleasuring Stevie in his 20-year-old horny mind.

He takes his wallet from his side pants pocket. He pulls out the folded paper from behind the two one-dollar bills. (O.K., he had gone to the Carnegie Library after listening to Carlos' crazy idea, just for the hell of it, just to look up what had happened that Easter Monday more than 60 years ago in the Dublin Post Office, and he had made a dupe of the proclamation.)

He unfolded the paper and read it (to himself), editing it to meet the occasion.

> "Puertorriqueños and puertorriqueñas: In the name of God, and from the dead generations from which she receives her old

tradition of nationhood, Puerto Rico, through us, summons her children to her flag and strikes for her freedom." (Skip the next few sentences.) "We declare the right of the people of Puerto Rico to the ownership of Puerto Rico, and to the unfettered control of Puerto Rican destinies, to be sovereign and indefeasible. The long usurpation of that right by a foreign people and government has not extinguished the right, nor can it ever be extinguished except by the destruction of the Puerto Rican people."

Here come the Riot Police, in bullet-proof black flak jackets, black helmets, visors covering their faces, carrying clubs and rifles, teargas canisters and bullets attached on belts across their chest and around their waist, orders shouted as they trot down the hilly streets leading to the post office. Here come the shots, the tear gas, the bullets flying through the air. And here come the M60 Patton tanks of the "foreign" U.S. Army (used near the end of the Vietnam War, he looked that up in the library), rolling down the hills and across the street in front of the post office, the 105mm guns spinning on the turrets to aim straight at the post office balcony . . .

He turns to go back down the staircase, but a coffee cart blocks his way. He looks at the silver urn holding coffee and he blinks and his nostrils quiver. An elderly woman with a large mole on her cheek and in a blue janitor-like dress sees Stevie eyeing the coffee pot. She fills a white plastic cup with the black liquid and holds it out to Stevie. "*Toma, m'ijo,*" she says.

Stevie takes, drinks, thanks the woman, twice, three times. He moves down the stairs and exits the building. He moves down to the harbor area of San Juan Bay. A huge luxury liner is pulling into a nearby dock. Along other docks, small boats transporting food, drink, etc. to and from nearby islands look like bathtub toys next to the monster liner.

He's shipping out, passing the ancient walls, the back patios of the houses huddled and piled above, passing the Governor's Mansion, the former home for nun's, passing the impenetrable El Morro into what appears to be the forever ocean. But, further on, there will be other islands. Other countries. Other worlds. It was up to Stevie Diaz to experience it all, in real-time and place—and in the head—and to put it all down on paper. Edit it into a life. A felt life, as real as the words on the pages allow.

Stevie Diaz, still dreaming at twenty.

ELEVEN

First Carmen started saying how she missed her little sister and although she didn't ask me outright, I could see she was trying to get me to say she could bring her sister to live with us. Which I didn't say. I thought the kid was better off with Rosa in the country.

Then she started with the cats. One evening when I came home from work there was a kitten in the kitchen licking milk from an ashtray. Carmen said she found it downstairs in the hallway, squealing its head off. *"Pobrecita,"* she said. "Her whore of a mother left her all alone."

A couple of nights later Carmen found another kitten in the hallway and brought it upstairs too. The word must have got around because by the time the week was out, Carmen had five kittens in the apartment, all of them she found in the hallway, she said. They were all over the place. One of them died after chewing up a tube of paint in the back room. Carmen put it in a wooden box and we had to go at night to a sentry box jutting out over the old Spanish wall by the San Juan Gate and throw the box and the cat into the sea below. I told her I didn't want no more pets and she should look for homes for the other four. Finally, I gave them to the Animal Rescue Society.

Then there were the bums and other "friends." She would bring them home for dinner. I made sure they left right after they ate. Once she brought home a drunken Chinaman who worked on a cargo ship that was in port. Carmen said she found the guy like the kittens, in the hallway. Two guys had tried to mug him in broad daylight, she said, and he fought them off but was hit on the head with something and he was lying in the hallway practically unconscious so she brought him upstairs to put a bandage over his eye. The Chinaman kept weaving back and forth and clenching his fists and glaring at me out of almost closed eyes like I was one of the muggers. I told Carmen to give him a sandwich and get him the hell out of the house and I went into the bedroom and slammed the door.

The last straw was Joanna.

When I came home one night, she was lying on the couch. Her shoes, which looked like ditch-diggers boots, were on the floor, next to half a dozen empty beer cans. Carmen said she was an old friend from New York who was here on a vacation and they met in the plaza by chance.

Joanna had short black hair combed in the back like a duck's behind. She had big liquidy brown eyes and pale skin that was yellowish under the eyes. A cigarette was always dangling from her thin colorless lips. She was wearing black pants and a blue work shirt and she talked tough. She kept calling Carmen a "cunt" and smiled every time she said it.

"I know this cunt for . . . hey, how many years I know you from, cunt? I met her one day at Seventy-Second Street and Broadway. She was all strung out and looked like a sick turd. I brung her home and took care of her. Remember, cunt?"

"Yeah, you was good to me, Mami," Carmen said. "We had a good t'ing until you started gettin' . . . you know."

"Whatta ya talkin'? You was the one that cut out 'cause I wouldn't let you turn tricks in the apartment wit' them assholes. All the perverts loved you, baby. What a cunt!"

Joanna flashed her teeth. They were horsey and white. "Yeah," Joanna said, "she would get all the freakos. Especially the dirty old men. She loved the old geezers. She got a thing for the moldy old salami, don't ya, cunt? Probably mental. Thinks she's humpin' her grandfather or something."

Carmen was smiling blissfully.

She was drinking beer and looked high. Joanna smiled at me, then widened her eyes like she noticed me for the first time. "Hey, no offense there. You ain't half as decrepit as some of the other johns she used to score with."

I grunted.

Joanna insisted on making us a spaghetti dinner. She made a real good sauce. After we ate, she said she would go buy some more beer. I told her, don't bother, I wanted to go to sleep early, I had a headache. She said I should go to sleep whenever I wanted, her and Carmen would drink the beer.

I looked at Carmen and she smiled and shrugged like she was telling me she couldn't say no to an old friend. I was gonna say something but decided not to. I went to sleep.

When I woke up the next morning, Carmen wasn't in the bed. I went to the bathroom and the door was locked. I thought Carmen was in there. After a couple of minutes, the toilet flushed, the door opened, and Joanna came out.

She was wearing a man's undershirt and panties. Her face was sickly white and damp and her eyes were half-shut.

"I just been pukin' my guts up," she said. "After we finished the beer, I got a bottle of rum and we finished that off too. I feel like shit on a stick." She went by me and into the back room where I do my painting and I heard her get into the bed I got there. I heard her tell Carmen, "Move over, gimme some room." Carmen moaned something I couldn't make out.

"I said move, cunt!" Joanna said and I heard bodies moving and springs bouncing and then a thump like someone fell onto the floor, and then Carmen's sleepy whine, more surprised than angry, "Hey, baby, what jou doin'?"

"I want some fuckin' room in this bed. I don't wanna go through this shit for the next two weeks."

"O.K., baby," Carmen said. "But don' think I got to shit jus' 'cause you say so."

I went to the room and threw the door open. "What the hell you think you doin' here?" I could feel my temples pounding hard.

"Eh, wha?" Joanna said.

"Get dressed and get the hell outta here!" I said.

"Hey, man," Joanna said, "what the fuck . . . ?"

"Get out!" I told her. "Fast!"

She got dressed and left. "So long, cunt," she said to Carmen. "See you next time you're back in the big apple."

Carmen was looking at Joanna, then at me with eyes like half-dollars.

"O.K.," I told her, trying to calm myself. "No more bringing here all the trash you find in the streets, you understand? I'm gonna give you one more chance, or I'm gonna throw you out too."

Carmen looked sheepish. "O.K., Papi. I'm sorry. I promise, no more."

She was good as her word. She didn't bring home nobody no more. We took a trip to the country again to see her sister and Rosa, and I even went with her to a salsa concert at Roberto Clemente Coliseum. It wasn't so bad as I expected. The music was loud, but so's everything in Puerto Rico when two or more people get together. There seemed to be something between the audience and the musicians that I ain't ever seen at any other musical show. Like there was something besides music being done there—the way the audience was reacting was as important as the music corning from the musicians.

We was close again. I decided to take Carmen up to New York the next week. I wanted her to see other things in life than what she's had until now. I told her the good things about New York. I didn't say, but that was where I got the chance to build a new life and make a good enough success in business, working for big diamond companies, polishing diamonds (which I learned in Amsterdam, see *The Autobiography of a Non-Famous Man*), and then having my own jewelry stores, and I met Miriam and she became my second wife and we had plenty of friends where we lived on the Upper West Side. Those pretty good successes were miracles to me. Miracles don't have to be Cecil B. De Mille spectaculars like the Red Sea parting. They can be average things. Especially if you thought you lost the will and the way to make these things happen. We had dinners for our friends and they had them too and we talked about serious things, but we were not always serious about them because the people who were born in America weren't going through what we refugees been through. Except, of course, for the Negro people who caught hell ten times over in America like the Jews of Europe.

In those first years, something in me came out to meet something in that city and both things seemed to get along real good. Life in New York was, as they said, a "rat race," even back then, but that didn't bother me, I was just overjoyed to be out and running again. And there were lots of really good things about New York then, as there still are, only less than before. What you learn in New York can make you both the hardest and the softest person around if you know what I mean.

My second marriage didn't last too long, just like the first one, but for different reasons, of course. Miriam escaped from Germany just in time, after her husband was killed by the Nazis, he wasn't even Jewish, but a philosophy professor at the university. She was really sweet and intelligent, though we both knew we couldn't love each other with the same passion as we did with our first spouses. We didn't have any kids, she couldn't become pregnant. Then something happened, I got too crazy about a lot of things, I won't go into that now, and we both decided it was best to split up for a while, which became permanent. In those last two years, all the good things about life in New York faded away for me. I was feeling depressed and wasn't seeing friends no more. Could I be "born again" in Puerto Rico? The Puerto Ricans I knew in New York were pretty decent people, and they worked hard. Forget about all that welfare crap they been blamed for. It was worth a try to keep surviving.

Anyway, when I was talking up our trip to New York, Carmen looked surprised like I wasn't serious. But she said, *"Si*. Anything you want, I'm gonna be wit' you*, mi amor."*

A couple of nights before we were going to go, it was about two in the morning, I was reading and Carmen was sleeping on the couch. She woke up and said she was hungry. There was almost nothing in the refrigerator so we decided to go to the all-night restaurant on Luna Street. After about a half hour, while Carmen was finishing up a goat fricassee and I had Cubano sandwich, Manny came into the restaurant. He seen us and came over to our table.

He made a bow to me." Nice seeing you again, Mr. Wolf." Then he said to Carmen: "Hey*, nena*, where you been?"

"I been with him," Carmen said, nodding and smiling at me.

"Yeah," Manny said. "My spies tell me they seen you and Mr. Wolf sittin' in the plaza eatin' ice cream. *Too much*, baby."

"I off the shit now," Carmen said.

"Yeah," Manny said. "Hey, that's great." Then he asked me: "Mind if I join you?"

I grunted, which was a yes for him and he sat.

"Hey, I'm sorry about that night, you know?" Manny said to me. "But I had an emergency at home. My kid has been sick the last few weeks. I gotta look out for her more than anything else, you know? I got lots of doctor bills too, so I got to find a couple of more steady customers since Carmen switched to ice cream." He gave his machine-gun laugh.

"Let's go," I said to Carmen. I called the waiter and got the check. "I hope your kid's O.K.," I told Manny. "And I hope you lose all your customers."

Manny's eyelids got heavy and his mouth got mean. Then he smiled. He pulled his head back. Another rapid-fire laugh.

"Hey, never happen, man," he said. "There's a junkie born here every minute. Nice seeing you again. Take care."

Seeing that sonovabitch again upset me, but he didn't seem to have no effect on Carmen. I told her that I thought he was scum and she nodded sleepily and put her head against my shoulder and said, "Yeah, baby, you right. But he's my cousin, you know? He's family, you know?"

The next night after dinner we went to the ice cream parlor again and bought ice cream and sat on a bench in the plaza across the street. We ate the ice cream, then Carmen went back across the street to buy cigarettes. Some kid came up to her and started talking to her. She kept nodding, then gave the kid some change. When she came back, I asked her what the kid wanted.

"He needed some money for the bus," Carmen said.

I didn't ask nothing further because I didn't think nothing more of it then.

When I came back from my store the next night, Carmen wasn't at the apartment. She wasn't home by eight o'clock.

Or ten.

Or by three in the morning.

TWELVE

Doris sat up in bed for the next hour, trying, unsuccessfully, to think of nothing. She dozed, her eyes shot open, her heart pounded; she dozed. She sprung up, grabbed her suitcase and Bessie's carrying case from the closet. She took the book she was reading, *Song of Solomon* by Toni Morrison. Bessie squealed and scratched, then finally agreed to get into her carrier. They were out of there by eight in the morning. The taxi she had called was waiting downstairs. She woke Paul. His eyes kept blinking him awake, but he smiled. "You did it, baby!" he said. "I'm so glad your back. This could, this *will* be the start of something big."

Paul said he had a friend with a small pickup truck who would take the rest of her stuff over when it was ready.

"No, no," Doris said. "This is just for the weekend."

"Hey. I want you here for all time," Paul said.

"Soon, but let's just work our way into it, weekend by weekend."

Paul took a deep breath, let it out, then nodded. "O.K., baby, weekend by weekend."

They kissed, the cab was waiting downstairs.

She actually got to work early. Wolf was late. He grunted when he saw her and Stevie and Don Alfonso and Bernice waiting in front of the store. He bent down, opened the padlock there, rolled up the metal shutter and unlocked the front door.

Wolf is often sour in the morning, but he usually loosens up as the day goes on and jokes a lot, and says interesting things. But he's been morose these last few days. As the workday was ending and Doris was bringing over some of the more expensive jewelry to be locked in the safe, she asked Wolf if everything was O.K.

"What everything?" he said.

"I mean, you, are you O.K.?"

"I'm . . . like I am."

Doris thought: Screw you.

Wolf got up from bending into the safe. He locked it, then he turned to Doris and said: "I'm sorry. I ain't so great, today."

"You wanna talk about it?"

"Dere's not much to talk about," Wolf said.

"You know I'm always here for you," Doris said.

"Yeah," said Wolf. He actually smiled at her. "You're a good person."

Was she? Who the hell knew? She patted Wolf on the shoulder, then gave him a hug and left. She walked down Fortaleza to the Plaza Colón, where she would wait for a bus to take her to her weekend "home." She'd get it together with Paul.

If that bastard John Jackson does come down here again, and if he . . . bothers her, she'll get a court order against him. If he lays a hand on her again, she'll go to the police. No, he'll know who to pay off. The courts here, at least, haven't been involved in any crooked stuff—yet. She'll get a lawyer and go to the court.

As for Wolf, he could take care of himself. He certainly has been doing it all these years.

Yeah, she had been closer than close to Wolf years ago. She'd just come down to the island and he kindly gave her a job and, well, other things happened.

She remembered one night when he took her to the Casals Festival at the University. Just before the intermission, the great Spanish cellist began playing *Kol Nidre,* the prayer recited by the Jews on the eve of *Yom Kippur.* She looked over to Wolf. There were tears in his eyes. Doris told Wolf she saw those tears. Wolf said: "My tears ain't got nothing to do with religion or God or prayers to heaven for forgiveness. The memories that hit my heart had to do with the Spanish Civil War and the Holocaust and the evil that people do here on earth." Then he smiled and kissed her on the cheek. Then he said: "We all got to stick together. We all *better* stick together."

O.K., Doris, you sort of owe him.

But he got his thanks from you.

Yeah, yeah, they appreciated one another.

Well if he needed something . . .

THIRTEEN

I knew that was it, Carmen wasn't coming back. Manny got her on drugs again, and now she's out selling her pussy so she could get money for dope.

I wanted to kill somebody. Preferably Manny. But if I found Carmen, I might have wrung her neck too. I sat out on the balcony all through the night, until it started getting light. I watched the sky turn pink and saw the sun come up over a dark cloud bank that looked like a piece of night that wasn't ready yet to go away. The birds woke in the trees. I sat there in the first light of day thinking dark thoughts. Then like my thoughts put it up there, I saw a wisp of dark cloud like smoke, and I remembered other days that began in pink and gold and ended in black, blotting out the sky.

I decided to try to get a couple hours sleep before going to work. I went in and lay down on the bed and I fell asleep right away. I had dreams like I ain't had for years. I woke drenched with sweat and tired as hell like I just been through all the things I dreamt about.

I lay there in bed with my breath coming short. The first thing I felt was an aching in my body like something was recently pulled out of my insides. Then I felt the sadness that comes from losing forever people you love. It's so deep it makes you feel helpless like a baby. Then I thought about Carmen leaving. She couldn't change. She was what she was.

Then I forced myself to get up and get ready to go to my store.

I stayed in the store until about three o'clock. I wasn't talking much to anyone and they knew better not to bother me. There was something angry growing inside me. It started coming out when this woman, she was about sixty-five and looked rich and was with a young oily-looking guy, she picked out an expensive pair of gold cufflinks for him and asked me how much was a sterling silver bracelet I recently made, it was from a Tibetan model with Sanskrit. I told her it was a hundred dollars. She said it was too much, she would give me seventy-five dollars for it. I told her, "This ain't the Casbah, lady, there ain't no bargaining in here." Then I said, "You'd pay a hundred dollars for a meal at one of the hotels for you and your boyfriend and soon you'd both go to the toilet. This is a work of art. It's worth more than what comes out of your ass, only you ain't smart enough to realize it."

She threw down the cufflinks and bracelet and left the store. I went up to the stock room on the second floor, to the desk I had up there, to the side drawer where I kept a bottle of Zebrowska vodka. I took a couple of gulps. When I went back downstairs I seen another wonderful "customer" in the store. It was Clyde, the husband of Bernice. He came inside because of what he didn't see. What he didn't see was me. If he had seen me he wouldn't have dared come through the door. Because he knows he would have got kicked out soon as he stepped a foot into the store, I done it before.

He wasn't alone. He had with him a bluish-black Great Dane that on all fours came up to his waist. And he wasn't a short guy. I heard Stevie tell him, "I'm sorry sir, but dogs are not allowed in the store." He pushed past Stevie. the dog right behind, its stub of a tail wagging above its high blue-black ass.

"Out of mah way, boy," he said. "Whar's Bernice? Whar is that bitch? Bernice! Get yo' cotton-pickin' ass over here!"

Bernice was behind the costume jewelry counter near the door. Her husband walked right past her. She tried to duck behind the counter, but because of the cast on her leg, she couldn't get down far enough.

"Aw, shit!" she said.

Her husband turned and so did the dog and it knocked a ceramic ashtray off a shelf. The ashtray broke into pieces.

"Get the hell out. And get that dog outta here!" I yelled.

He turned to me. Something wavered in his eyes like he thought he should listen to me. But he also looked angry, and drunk. Then he told me with his eyes he wasn't going no place just because I said so. He was wearing a tee shirt that looked like it ain't been off his back in a month and he had a week's growth of beard. He opened his mouth and let out a loud deep belch. Then he looked past me and yelled: "Ber-r-r-nice, bitch, bitch!"

"Hi, Clyde, honey," Bernice said in a high sugary voice and waved her fingers at him like a little girl. Her smile twitched.

"Hi, Clyde, honey." Her husband imitated her voice and waved his fingers at her. "You gonna '*hi, honey*' me when ah break yo' other leg, bitch? Huh? You gonna do that then?"

Bernice was still smiling, but her whole face was twitching now. She didn't say nothing.

I went towards Clyde. He grabbed a heavy Haitian walking stick from a rack and ran around a stand of shelves and down another aisle and pulled the stick back like a baseball bat and measured Bernice's head.

"You take one mo' step," he said, "and I'll break open her head grapefruit."

I froze. So did everybody else in the store, including the tourists. I could feel my blood pressure rising.

"So since you been gone, bitch," Clyde said to Bernice, "ain't you at least missed Marvin here?" He patted the dog hard against its body. "Why don't you say, 'Hi Marvin, honey' too, huh?"

Bernice looked around with her shaky smile like she was telling everyone they're going to get a kick out of what was coming next. Her face was deep red under her freckles.

Her husband cracked the stick against the floor. "Say, 'Hi, Marvin, honey' 'fore I bust this fuckin' stick over yo' head. Say it!"

"Hi, Marvin, honey," Bernice said. The dog cocked its head.

"Now you tell Marvin here how much you missed him. Tell him!"

"I missed you much, Marvin," Bernice said.

"That's enough," I shouted. Get the hell . . ."

"Shut up sonovabitch," Clyde yelled at me. He swung the stick across a shelf and knocked to the ground a whole bunch of Don Quixotes from Russia. Luckily, they were cast iron, they didn't break. Then he held the stick with both hands over his head. "Ah swear to Christ ah will break this bitch's head wide open, you say one mo' motherfuckin' word!"

Now he turned to the dog. "Get up here, Marvin, and give yo' mama a kiss." He patted the counter and the dog put its front paws on it. It was panting, its long pink tongue hanging out and saliva rolling off onto the counter.

"Come on, Bernice, you bitch," Clyde said, "swap spits with ol' Marvin here. Come on, bitch. Do it!"

Bernice looked at us and shrugged like this was just a little family joke, we shouldn't take it too serious. Then she pushed her face to the dog and he licked it.

"In the mouth!" Clyde yelled. "Put yo' tongue in Marvin's mouth. Put it raht in there."

Bernice squeezed shut her eyes and puckered her lips and let the dog lick them. She pulled away and wiped her mouth. "Ah cain't, honey," she said.

"What I should have you be doin'," he said, "is suckin' off ol' Marvin. Just like you was doin' to that other animal, that guy upstairs, when I catched you that night. Ain't that what you was doin'? Ain't it?"

"Honey, I . . ."

"Say it! Say, 'I was suckin' off a animal when Clyde catched me.' Say it or you ain't never goin' to say anything again."

Bernice said what he wanted her to. Then he turned and said to everyone in the store: "See, ah got a wife which sucks and fucks animals. And that's how she treats me. Like a dawg. To her, I ain't no better than a dawg." There were tears in his eyes. He shook his head like it was his fault for being too nice. "She thinks more of Marvin here than she does of me. Don't she, ol' fella? Huh, now?"

The dog had its front paws on Clyde's shoulders, trying to lick his face. Clyde said to the dog: "She likes you better 'an she do me, you know that Marvin? That 'cause you tonguin' her better? Are you tonguin' her, boy? Cain't ah even trust mah little ol' doggie?"

Clyde pushed the dog's paws off his shoulders and he whacked the stick hard against the dog's side and the dog yelped and howled and bolted into a stand and everything went flying and crashing to the ground. The dog started galloping around the store, breaking more things and smashing into a jewelry counter and the shoppers who were frozen looking at what was going on now were screaming and yelling and running for the door.

I ran behind Bernice's husband and kicked him hard as I could in the ass and he went flying to the ground and the Haitian walking stick went clattering across the floor and the dog jumped over Clyde and dashed out the door.

I picked up the hand-carved Haitian walking stick and banged it on the floor. "Get the hell out of here, you bastard," I told Clyde. "And if you ever come back, I'll have you put in jail, you no-good rotten sonovabitch bastard!" I banged the stick on the floor again.

Clyde gave me a sheepish smile and started toward the door.

"Have a good day, Clyde," Bernice said.

I turned to her. "You too," I yelled. "I don't want to see you or your boyfriends no more. You understand? Get the hell out of here."

Bernice hobbled around the counter. "Listen, Mr. Wolf, it wasn't my f . . ."

"Out! Out!" I pointed to the door and she limped out. I was sweating and dizzy and out of breath.

I locked the door, then started picking up things. Stevie, Carlos, and Don Alfonso helped me. After about thirty minutes, we got almost everything back in shape. Then I decided to close the store.

I went back to the apartment. I went to the toilet about five times. I had diarrhea. I told myself Carmen left because somehow that sonovabitch Manny made her leave. I convinced myself that was the reason. I would go out and find her and bring her back, which was what she wanted. I decided to get some rest before I went looking for her. I fell asleep right away, and again I had some beautiful dreams, which I didn't remember when I woke up. But what stayed with me was the depression. I felt I was dying inside.

I knew Carmen didn't leave because Manny made her. But because she wanted to. She was a junkie and a whore. She couldn't get used to any other kind of life.

I fell asleep, woke like I got a shock, slept, was shocked again.

I took some drinks from the vodka bottle I had in the freezer. I staggered back to the bed, slept, got up, took another drink, went back to bed. I wasn't going no place tonight.

FOURTEEN

Stevie sat on a bench in Plaza San José, to the right of Ponce de León, who stood high on a pedestal and pointed a bronze finger to . . . wherever. Behind the Fountain of Youth seeker was the 16th Century San José Church, one of the oldest in the hemisphere. He didn't find historically worshipful stuff like this in the Bronx (except maybe for the Yankee Stadium.)

It was after work, the sky was a dusky purple and the lampposts in the plaza were lit. Stevie had walked up to the plaza to his favorite bench; then out from his black shoulder bag came the marble-covered school notebook. He also extracted the half of the Cubano sandwich from lunch. Left in the bag was the empty, earlier-Pepsi filled thermos bottle, ballpoints, and a hardcover of *Lord Jim,* parts of which he wanted to read again, especially the storm at sea—just to see again how Conrad does it, not to copy for the storm in his own novel—*you better not!*—before returning the book to Mr. Wolf.

He often wrote some pages here, typed them up later at home. This was his Paris café.

Next chapter. Start with his dream, dress it up a bit:

> "We were in a monster storm that seemed to explode all around us. The ship was lifted—it seemed the bow was rising vertically, into the air, where she quivered like the top floors of a building caught in an earthquake, then plunged down, miraculously all in one piece, with a crashing roar. It happened again and again and each time the ship rose shuddering above the giant waves, my tugging and twisting gut told me she was going to break up in the next plunge down into the boiling waters . . .

"Hey, what's up, *mi pana?*"

It was Carlos, from the store.

"Just writing a few things down," Stevie said, closing his notebook.

"Move over," Carlos said. "We're meeting here for dinner, at *El Patio de Sam*." He motioned with his head to the restaurant on the other side of the plaza, then sat next to Stevie. He stared at the notebook. Stevie put it back into his shoulder bag.

"You writing your memoirs?"

"Well . . . sort of."

"Your life in New York, before returning to the homeland?"

What the fuck, he doesn't have to keep it a secret. "I'm writing a novel."

Carlos widened his eyes, pulled his long head back and looked at Stevie as though he was seeing him for the first time. "Hey, that's great. What's it about?"

Stevie took a deep breath. "It's about a young Puerto Rican who goes to sea on a British ship, in the early 1900s. You know, the adventures he has on the different islands they go to, mostly British colonies. I looked up some stuff and you see how the colonialized "natives" were treated then, it may have been in a different style, but not all that different from the U.S. and its relations with Puerto Rico. An older guy who is a lifetime seaman—he's the 'father' the cabin boy never really had—he takes him around to teach him about the world and . . ."

"So why," Carlos interrupted, "do you want to write about the colonialism of yesterday? Why don't you write about what's happening today, here, *now*? Write about the PR government, which is really run from Washington, kicking poor people off land they always lived on because some billionaire U.S. corporation that stole the land for pennies years ago wants to build luxury hotels for rich tourists there. Write about those two young guys who were convinced by that fuckin' traitor who was really a cop to blow up the communications towers on the Cerro Maravilla mountaintop as a symbol for Puerto Rico's independence and the young guys fell into the trap and the cops ambushed and murdered them. Write about the fuckin' U.S. Navy doing bombing exercises on Puerto Rico islands where people live. Or the fuckin' FBI teaming up with Cuban exile assholes to get rid of anyone who works for the island\s independence. Write about what's really happening today, not what you make up in your head happened a long time ago."

Stevie took a deep breath. "Yeah, but for me, what happens in novels is what happens to people at any time in any place and from the experiences you make up, you can reach a deep truth that says something about . . ."

"About what's in your head, not what was, is, really going on. You can fantasize your ass off, but don't try to pass it off as some profound statement on the real-life truth of the matter. Give the reader the facts, man, the facts! Let them see what's *really* going on in the here and now. Tell them how fucked up the island is because of the fuckin' colonial policy that no one in Washington will admit to!" Then Carlos added: "Have you ever been to sea?"

"Well, not really, but . . ."

"So how could you possibly . . . ?"

"I don't think that someone who writes a novel has to have had the exact experiences he's writing about. Steinbeck was never an Okie. Dante was never in hell. If you have a strong enough, umh . . . a strong imagination, a deep enough feeling for people and what they crave and love and . . ."

"But I don't want to read about what's only in *your* head. Even in a novel, I want to read about the truth of something that someone knows about first-hand, not off the top of . . ."

"Papi! Papi!" A boy and girl, both about three or four and both dressed in sailor suits, ran up to Carlos and jump into his long-armed embrace. A pretty young woman in a sleeveless white blouse and an ankle-length flowery skirt stood behind them smiling.

"So you made it," said Carlos. He introduced Marta, the wife Stevie didn't know Carlos had, and the twins, Juan and Juanita.

"The traffic was maddening. We were stuck in the bus close to an hour. But we did get here," Marta said with a gleaming smile.

Carlos looked deep into his wife's eyes and gave her a long-toothed smile, "Well, we're going to have a great dinner!" He turned to Stevie with the smile still on his face and said: "Hey, man, you do what you got to do. I'm just a grouch." He gave Stevie an *abrazo*, then took his kids' hands and led them across the plaza, his wife alongside, laughing at something.

So Carlos, the hard-ass revolutionary, is also, a warm family man. Or maybe he's faking it. Faking what? Who the hell knows?

Everyfriggintime he judges someone or something, another thing happens to put a new look on the people and the events.

He's got to get something like that into his novel.

FIFTEEN

I opened the store the next morning, stayed about an hour, then told Don Alfonso to take charge, I still wasn't feeling good, Back to bed, back to the toilet, back to bed. I took aspirins and a sleeping pill.

Then, finally, I got up when the sun was going down. I was actually feeling hungry. I went to the *Siglo XX* Cuban restaurant around the corner and had some *sopa de pollo* (chicken soup) and I was feeling better. Then I went to the Malomundo bar for my Polish vodka, I didn't want to drink at home by myself.

As usual, the place was crowded. Most of the regulars were there. The guy they called Overcoat was nursing a beer at a table, hunched down in his long-frayed coat like he just came in from a winter storm. He wears the coat in all weather, even though the temperature almost never goes below seventy degrees. Around the smoky bar were a lot of blurry, blotched faces. There were also some tourists there and a group of seamen yelling at each other in German.

And guess who else was there, right in the middle of the floor, doing a solo dance to a rock and roll song coming from the jukebox? It was Bernice. She was hobbling around on her cast, clumsily jerking her hips and ass, moving her head around in circles and flapping her arms. She looked like a spastic trying to cross the floor.

I went to a corner table and got a vodka. I downed it and ordered another. Bernice finished her dance and limped back to the bar. She hopped up on a stool next to a short heavy-set guy in an army uniform and put her arm around his shoulders.

"How are you doin', sergeant?" she said.

The soldier nodded slowly like he was thinking about it. He had a short, thick neck and the back of his head was flat.

Bernice took a long drink from her glass, then said to everyone at the bar: "How y'all doin'? Ah hope y'all havin' a nice day. Ah sho' as hell am." She drained her glass, ordered another, held it up to toast everyone at the bar, then turned to the tables and saw me.

"Why look who's there," she said. "Why it's Mr. Wolf," like we ain't seen each other for a long time, instead of just yesterday when I fired her. "Hi, Mr. Wolf. Long time, no see," she said with a wink.

I grunted and she smiled wide, showing me her long yellow teeth. She worked herself down from the stool, her arm still around the sergeant's neck, forcing him off his stool too. "Come on over here, sergeant, and say hello to Mr. Wolf, my boss. Even though I ain't working for him no more, I still think of him as *my* boss."

She hobbled over to my table carrying her drink, and the sergeant reluctantly followed. They stood there, looking down at me. Bernice, wobbling and holding tight to the soldier's arm, said: "Mr. Wolf, I'd like you to meet Sergeant Pete Gonzalez, who's just a fabulous fella. Throw the man a highball, sergeant. Give him a salute!"

The sergeant forced a smile and shook my hand. He had a wide jowly face with small features. "A pleasure to make your acquaintance, sir, I'm sure," he said.

Bernice screwed up her eyes like she was suddenly angry. The sergeant smiled embarrassed at me, then gave me a half-hearted salute. Then he winked at me.

"Mind if we join you?" Bernice asked.

I grunted again. Bernice sat and the sergeant did too. He had an uncomfortable grin on his face. I drank my vodka down and ordered another one.

"Listen, Mr. Wolf," Bernice said, "I'm sorry about what happened earlier today. I really am. What a terrible thing for that man to do, upsettin' your store like that and all. I was so ashamed."

She pouted and looked down and away. Then, slowly, she looked up at me and smiled like a little girl who wanted something but was too bashful to ask for it. She looked at me like that, with her head bent off to the side and her eyes crinkling up at me and that stupid smile on her face.

"What is it already?"

"I was just thinking, Mr. Wolf, sir," she said in a tiny voice, "do you think it's possible . . . could you . . . would I possibly be able to get my job back?" The smile was twitching.

I looked at her a long time and she bit her lower lip like she was nervous and her whole life depended on my answer. Which was bullshit and I was about to tell her she was too much of a pain in the ass with all her boyfriends and that moron of a husband she had. She's a trouble-maker, but she knew the merchandise. I didn't want to start looking for another worker, I had other things on my mind.

"You can come back," I said, "so long as there ain't no more trouble there from your visitors. And I mean no more! Because next time, he's going to jail and you're . . ."

"No more trouble, Mr. Wolf, I promise you. None at all. No trouble, no trouble."

She was saying all this in her fawning little voice. But then her voice got louder and it got meaner and she tightened up her mouth and said: "There ain't gonna be no more trouble because if that miserable sonovabitch ever gives me a hard time again I got mah warrior here to kick ass! Don't I, lover?"

The sergeant cracked his knuckles. "I don't support a man bad-mouthing or beating a woman," he said. "*Any* woman. I think that that woman could be somebody's sister or mother and that gets me angrier than hell. I'll go after any bastard, no matter what his size, he could be big as a deuce and a half or small as a turd, any bastard who beats or bad-mouths a woman is going to hear from me. That's one of the rules I live by. You beat or bad-mouth a woman, you got trouble from me." He cracked his knuckles again.

"You mah tiger," Bernice said, putting her arm around the sergeant's shoulder and pulling his head toward hers and sticking her tongue deep into his ear.

"Hey, honey," he said. "Cut it out! Not here."

She smiled like a little girl again. "Sorry 'bout that, lover. But ever since I met you just a couple hours ago, I can't keep offa you."

"Yeah; well, just control yourself," the sergeant said. He looked uncomfortable. But then he winked at me again.

Bernice finished her drink, then let out a long, deep belch. She lowered her eyes and tapped her chest. "'scuse me." Then she turned to the bar and shouted, "Hey, Mitzi, bring us another round."

"*Ja, ja,*" said Mitzi, the bartender, she's from Germany and got a face like the Russian Army marched over it—a flat crooked nose, swollen looking cheeks, a chin pointed one way, her mouth twisted down the other way. She's got nice eyes though, big and dark. "Hold your horses," she said, "or your boyfriend's *schwanz*. Whichever you want to hold."

The German seamen at the bar laughed loud and shouted in German to Mitzi and she answered them.

Then Bernice's husband Clyde came into the bar.

This time he looked different. He was wearing a clean tee shirt and was shaven and his hair was wet and combed and looked like it just been cut. If he seen Bernice, he didn't let on. He went right to the bar and sat with his back towards us. But there was a mirror behind the bar and he could see our table in it.

Bernice sat up, looked real serious and elbowed the sergeant. "That's him," she said excited. "That's Clyde Burns." She said his name loud, but he didn't turn. "Yeah," Bernice said louder, "that's him all right. That's the sonovabitch that broke mah leg, that's Clyde Virgil Burns who humiliated me some more in front of my co-workers just a couple of hours ago."

Clyde still didn't turn. He ordered a drink.

Sergeant González was looking real mean at Clyde's back. Then he put a hand on Bernice's arm. "Calm down, honey," he said. "We don't want no scene here. I'm a black belt in judo and my hands are considered deadly weapons. He comes over to the table, I'm liable to kill or cripple him."

"Wowee!" said Bernice. "That would suit me just fine! You hear that, Mr. Clyde Virgil Burns? This man sittin' raht aside me is trained to kill. With his hands! Ooo-wee!"

"Cool it, baby!" The sergeant wasn't looking too happy.

I was on my fourth or fifth vodka and my head started spinning and I leaned it against the wall. Bernice got up and started stumbling and stomping around again to music coming from the jukebox. She was moving closer and closer to Clyde and then she brushed against him and began cackling and Clyde hunched the back of his shoulders into his neck like a turtle trying to get into its shell, and the sergeant was sitting there with a sad look on his face.

Then I saw the stripes on the sergeant's sleeve inside my head; they turned upside down and became birds and they were flying against a bright blue sky and below there was a field of yellow and blue flowers and I was walking across the field with a knapsack on my back and inside the knapsack was everything I owned in life and my feet were aching from all the walking I was doing from country to country and the smell of the flowers and the field went deep inside me. But then the sky got red and the field became one long wide muddy ditch and everywhere there were naked bodies, they were dead or dying, moaning and crying and vomiting and covered with blood and slimy mud and their own shit, and I was choked by another smell, this one sweet and sickening and it became stronger and sweeter and more sickening, it clogged my head and gave me a terrific pain, first between my eyes, then at the temples, then building up to the top of my head, which felt like it was going to blow off—and then the song came crashing through and exploded inside my head and I jumped out of my chair and yelled out, "Shut up with that goddamn song!"

The four German seamen at the end of the bar stopped singing. They were young guys with thin, sort of innocent faces. Everyone was looking at me. Then the Germans started singing again, this time louder and staring straight at me. It was a patriotic song and hearing the German words again sung like that was enough to drive me nearly crazy. "Shut up with that pigshit already!" This time I hollered it in German.

They kept on singing, and then I saw Bernice grab the sergeant by the back of the head and pull his head towards her and she gave him a long moaning kiss and then a glass smashed on the floor and Clyde was off his stool.

Clyde came across the floor, flipped over the table and glasses went flying and crashing to the ground. Bernice, the sergeant and me jumped up and tried to get out of the way. Clyde pulled his arm back, ready to punch, whoever, and Mitzi came running from behind the bar with a big wooden club that she swatted against Clyde's back and I pushed past the forward-staggering Clyde and stumbled out of the bar.

My head was spinning. I leaned against a parked car for a few moments. Then I went to the corner to look for a taxi to take me to the Condado. After a few minutes, a cab came by.

Ashford Avenue was crowded with tourists and hookers and others and I walked up and down from the Sheraton Hotel to the Dos Hermanos Bridge looking for Carmen. But she wasn't there selling her pussy. I went through hotel lobbies and looked at the bars in the lobby and in the lounges and the casinos. Still no Carmen.

I went back to one of the casinos and started playing blackjack and stayed for about an hour. I lost a hundred bucks. I couldn't concentrate. Then I left and went back up and down Ashford and into the lobbies and lounges and other casinos again. Carmen wasn't nowhere.

I took a taxi to the waterfront and started going through the bars there. I had a couple of drinks in each place and soon my head was spinning again. I went into a dive called The Latin Quarters. It was a long, low-lit place with some tables in the back and a jukebox, which was playing a romantic song in Spanish. At the bar, a couple of hookers sat on stools with their heads on their crossed arms. None of them was Carmen. I left.

I had to find Carmen and rescue her because when I saved her I was saving my beautiful Sarah, and I was saving Rachel, and millions of others, not to mention myself. That was my drunken-self talking to me.

I couldn't find a cab and walked to Old San Juan, then went to the all-night restaurant on Luna Street. The underbelly was there like always. But not Carmen. I had an omelet and coffee, then went home. The sky was starting to get light.

When I got to my apartment, the front door was wide open. There was no lock in the door, just a hole with wood scraped and chipped away around the hole. Then I saw the lock. It was on the floor behind the door.

The burglars didn't get much. How could they? I didn't have nothing of value for them, not even a TV. My hi-fi was old and chipped, they couldn't have gotten more than a couple of dollars for it and it was so bulky, they left it. They took a cheap portable radio and some clothes, mine and Carmen's.

But it's always good to have something more for burglars to take. Because if they don't think they got enough, they get angry. And do things. Like shit in your bed. Which wouldn't have been so bad because what those sonsovbitch bastards did is they smashed my Mozart records and they ripped up my books.

And then I saw they did worse.

I had three of my paintings hanging in my living room. They were called "Persecution" and "Execution" and "Resurrection." They slashed with a knife all three paintings. I went into the bedroom. They cut up the two paintings hanging there too. Then I ran into the room in the back I use as a studio. I was breathing heavy and my heart was punching into my chest. I had over twenty paintings stacked there. And the painting of Carmen was there too.

They slashed them. All of them. They slashed Carmen's portrait to pieces.

I went back to the living room and sat in my old leather armchair and put my head back and stared at the ceiling fan. I didn't put the fan on. The windows were shut. I sat there with the sweat rolling down my body. What they did was worse than if they stole everything I ever owned.

First, I cursed the landlord for not fixing the lock on the downstairs door, he's been told about it a hundred times. Then I cursed myself for not coming home all night. Those sonsovbitches know when you're out.

And inside me it felt like those terrible years. And then with a rush of panic, I thought: the last thirty-five years were a short peaceful nap, and the wide-awake nightmare is beginning again.

SIXTEEN

A couple of nights ago, what she was scared about, it happened. John Jackson came to town. It took him just a couple of days to find his still-legal wife, Doris. He actually saw an ad in *The San Juan Star* about the Paul Warren Quartet, appearing nighty (except Mondays) at Mimi's bar-restaurant in Ocean Park, and featuring Doris Jackson, vocals.

He snuck in during her last performance Saturday (about 1 a.m.), stood at the crowded bar, then, as soon as she left the tiny stage, came up to her, applauding.

"You sound better than ever, Ms. Jackson," he said. "You are Billie, some Sarah, and even Ella on that last scat. You are finally ready for the big time—if that is where you want to go."

Apparently, John Jackson still did not use contractions when he spoke. He didn't seem drunk. His wavy once-black-black hair was now salt-and-peppery, and so was his mustache. That mouth, still swollen-lipped and somewhat pouty, the eyes black and sparkly, as always. He wore a long-sleeved light blue guayabera—just like the other Latinos, which he wasn't—and his once black plastic glasses were now replaced by wire-rims. Doris looked around for Paul. It was a reflex, she couldn't help it. Paul was still at the piano, talking to Mimi, the false-polite old hag who owned the club and more than once tried to short him and the group on their promised salaries.

O.K. Doris, confront John Jackson.

"What do you want, from me? Haven't we broken it off, for good?"

"Hey, baby, I am here for a short vacation and of course I am going to look you up. You were so much a part, we were so much a part, our lives were entwined. I am sure that you remember. By the by, how come you disconnected your telephone?"

"I moved," Doris said. "I don't have my own phone."

"You want to give me another number to get in touch with you?

"No, not right now."

"Look, I know, I have not always been a good guy with you. In fact, at times, I have been a mean bastard. I sort of knew it then and I certainly know it now, since I've been . . . well, in therapy. See, I realize that I had this—this thing that made me feel that I couldn't trust women because my mother, well I loved her, but, you see, well, she was not always on the up and up with me, and with others, and . . . well . . . O.K., enough of the John Jackson psychodrama. What I want now is to make it up to you. I want to say over and over that I apologize. And that . . . that, on my part, there has always been love. Yeah, I was a cruel bastard, but the love never left. It's always been there. And seeing you tonight, dear Doris, it is, I know, still there. So, you know . . ."

Blame the mother. Yeah, sure, that's why you became such a bastard to women. How about just realizing you weren't man enough to realize the way you acted had everything to do with you?

Doris stopped listening. But she kept looking. The mystery in those dark dark eyes were still there; even, now, a sort of hurt tenderness. Oh, bullshit! How come there was no hate there, as there was in those other terrible days and nights?

Doris, you had hated that bastard –and, of course, given you as you—had loved him too.

Then she said: "I'm trying to build a new life, John."

"So, my dear, am I."

"Well, we are going to each have to do it by ourselves. I want you, John, to leave me alone."

John Jackson looked around at the halfway rundown bar. His chest shook, as though he were trying to hold in a laugh. He took out a handkerchief from his back pocket and wiped his face.

"Look, Doris, all I am asking is one more chance. How about we meet, well, the first night you have off, or early in the evening, or for lunch, or even for an early breakfast. Whenever you have some free time. We will get a get a great lobster dinner at your favorite restaurant in Isla Verde—*Atlantica*. right? We will go to a casino out there, you can be my lucky charm as I wipe out the house at the dice table. Then we will dance in the night club there and share a bottle of Remy and retire to our room in the hotel—just like in the old days. And I . . . I . . . Whatever you want. Like in the old days."

Like in the old days. How long would it take before he "discovered" something about the way she walked or talked or dressed or breathed that sent him into a non-lawyerly rage, so that he could use other bodily parts like his fists, his feet, and even what's in the vicinity like his belt, and once a slab of wood, shouting at her to apologize, which sometimes she had done—to stop the beatings—but other times she had refused, which hardened his rage.

Doris turned again to Paul, who was gathering up the sheet music he used to accompany her.

Ready?" she asked.

He nodded and winked.

She turned back to John Jackson. "I'm sorry," she said. "I have a new life now."

John Jackson slowly nodded. He gave Doris a sour smile. "Some things," he said, "can\t ever, won't ever, change."

"Yeah?"

"Yeah. I will see you around, *mi amor.*" John Jackson turned and walked quickly out of the bar.

Paul came up to Doris and took her hand. "Who was that you were talking to?"

"One of my fans," Doris said.

SEVENTEEN

The next morning, I went to the locksmith and had a new lock put on my door. Then I went to the store. I managed to stick it out all day. I kept thinking I needed a gun. I wasn't gonna wait the months it takes to get a legal permit. I needed protection right away.

And I kept thinking about Carmen, how I felt something was torn out from inside me.

After work, I took a long nap and woke up at ten and made myself an omelet, then went to the Condado again to look for Carmen. I made the same rounds up and down Ashford Avenue and in the casinos and bars and lounges, but again I couldn't find her. Instead of going to the waterfront bars again, I stayed in the casinos. I managed to lose a couple of hundred dollars.

At about three in the morning, I went to the all-night restaurant in Old San Juan. Carmen wasn't there. But Manny was. This time it was me who went over to his table and sat. He gave me a warm hello like we was old friends. Manny wasn't alone. With him was a gorilla of a guy with tattooed arms bulging out of a black T-shirt, a forehead that sloped back under black wavy hair, small mean eyes and a lot of empty spaces between his teeth. He didn't look too smart. Manny didn't bother to introduce the gorilla, who was ripping into a steak.

"Where's Carmen?" I said.

"I ain't seen her since the night with you a couple of nights ago," Manny said. "Ain't she staying with you?"

Manny seen something happening in my face and he raised his hands in front of his chest, palms out with the fingers spread apart and he shrugged. "Hey, man, I'm telling you the truth. *La Verdad.*

I ain't seen that bitch since that night." I looked at him and Manny shrugged again. He went back to his chicken and rice.

I didn't believe him. Why should I have? I'd find out later if he was lying. Right now I needed that sonovabitch.

I said to him: "I need a gun."

Manny looked up, surprised as hell. He looked at me and nodded slowly and a small smile came onto his face like he was learning something new about me. "You want to get rid of someone?" he said, looking happy at the prospect.

"My apartment was broken into last night," I said. "I need a gun for protection against robbers. There ain't no other reason." I felt my face getting red.

"Yeah," Manny said. He took a long swig of beer. Then he said: "Hey, in case you got something special in mind, Hector here can help you out."

Hector, the gorilla, looked at me with his little mean eyes and gave me a smile. There was some kind of dumb expectancy in the smile.

Manny said, "Hector, he can do any kind of job for you. We'll give you a good price."

Hector was pouring rice and beans on the steak plate and gobbling it all down. Without looking up from his food, he nodded. Then with his mouth still full, he said: "I'll take care of any guy you want, my friend. You see, I got this steel plate in my head"—he looked up and tapped his left temple—"which I got from being in Nam. You see, I knock of£ these guys and if I get caught I tell the judge about the steel plate and about all the gooks I killed for my country and how I get these terrible pains in my head and they put me away for a couple of months and then I'm out again. It happened like that before. Right, Manny?"

"That's right," Manny said.

Hector smiled and shrugged like he was saying how easy the whole thing would be. Then he caught the waiter by the arm and ordered a fried chicken.

"I wanna buy a gun for my own protection," I told Manny. "You can help me get one or you can't?"

"Sure," Manny said. "No sweat on that, Wolf. But I can't do nothing for you tonight. I'll pick you up tomorrow at noon in the Plaza Colón and we'll do a deal, O.K.?"

"Yeah, O.K.," I said.

The waiter brought Hector's chicken and he picked up a leg and started chewing it to pieces. There was a pitcher of water on the table, but no glasses. He looked at the pitcher, then for the waiter.

"I need a glass," he said.

"Don't be bashful," Manny told him. "Drink the water from the pitcher."

Hector's gorilla face lit up. He picked up the pitcher with one hand and drank from it and water ran down onto his shirt and pants.

"What a fuckin' animal!" Manny said.

Hector grinned.

I left.

I opened the store the next morning, then left at noon, saying I didn't feel good again. I went down to the plaza and waited for an hour and started leaving a couple of times; then Manny finally showed up. He pulled up in an old rusty blue Chevrolet with bumpers twisted like pretzels. His sunglasses blotted out his eyes. His skin was real pale in the sunlight and the scars made his face look like one of those close-up pictures of the moon. I got in and the car squealed away like we were making a getaway from the scene of a crime.

Manny had the radio on full blast and the music was giving me a headache.

"Turn that noise down already!" I said.

"What's the matter, man, don't you dig salsa?"

"When it's that loud," I said, "it ain't nothing but noise."

I turned the radio down. Manny turned it back up. I turned it down again. He turned it up. I turned it off. He gave me one of his machine-gun cackles.

We drove down near the Caribe Hilton, then doubled around and started back to the Old City along the oceanfront road.

Manny pulled off the road near Escambron beach, then drove to the parking area and down to a spot that looked over the ocean. He looked around to make sure we were the only ones in the immediate area. Outside, the wind slapped against the palm trees. The leaves waved at us. A finger-sized freighter sat far out on the ocean.

Manny reached into the glove compartment and pulled out a gray plastic bag. He opened the bag and took out a pistol which he said was a snub-nosed thirty-eight. It had a pearl handle and was nickel-plated. He handed it to me. It felt good, not too heavy.

"You can off someone up to twenty-five yards with that," Manny said.

"How much is it?"

His face got real serious. "It's a Smith-Wesson. The *best*. I don't deal in inferior pieces. If I did, I could get you a thirty-eight from Brazil for half the price, it would probably blow up in your hand. But I wouldn't do that. I only sell the best pieces available. I'll throw in a few boxes of steel-jacketed dum-dums all for, say, three and a half bills."

"Three hundred fifty dollars?"

"That's the ticket," Manny said. "It's a good deal, Wolf."

He was probably charging me at least double for a second- or third-hand gun. But I wasn't going to quibble. I wanted to get out of there. I gave Manny the money and put the gun and boxes of bullets into an attaché case I brought along.

Manny counted out the money real quick. He saw the way I was looking and smiled. "I used to be a bank teller," he said, "before they caught me taking home samples." He nodded and put out his hand. "Good doing business with you, Mr. Wolf."

"I bought your gun," I said, "but I don't have to shake your hand."

Manny looked hard at me, then threw back his head for another machine-gun cackle. "I really like your style."

I started to get out of the car.

"Hey, where you going? I'll drive you," Manny said.

"No you won't," I said. "I need some fresh air."

"Whatever you say," Manny said.

I walked across the parking area and Manny zoomed the car past me, the tires kicking up pebbles. I got back on the ocean road and walked into Old San Juan.

I went back to my apartment and sat in my leather arm chair and put the attaché case on my lap. I opened it and took out the gun and held it in front of me. I pulled the trigger. It clicked. I put the gun back in the case and put the case in the bedroom closet. Then I went into the living room and opened the doors that led to the balcony. I stepped out on the balcony and watched the Saturday shoppers corning into the Old City on the buses pulling into the plaza. I thought about Carmen sitting out there with me. I felt a deep pang. My breath got short. I punched my fist down on the wooden balcony rail.

I went inside. The hell with her.

I spent the rest of the day sitting in the leather chair. Thinking. About Carmen.

That night, and the next six nights, I spent in the casinos, mostly losing. During the days, I was in and out of my store, being short with the customers and the help.

I was moving around like a zombie. I wasn't feeling too good physically either. I had a lot of diarrhea and was weak and dizzy.

Doris Jackson was concerned and came to my apartment after work several days to "keep you from falling to pieces." She cooked dinners and made sure I went to bed at a reasonable hour—I got up later to sit around and stare—and part of it, at least, was like those early years between us. Before leaving at about eight or nine, she kissed me good night, but that was all.

I remembered when, years and years ago, she came into my store and asked if there were any job openings. She was an attractive woman and seemed smart and sympathetic (that was before she started drinking real heavy), so I hired her.

When she showed up, she was a good worker, making jokes with the customers and laughing like she didn't have a care in the world. When old Jewish tourists came into the store, she joked with them with Yiddish words. She knew how to make jokes in Spanish too. Happy-go-lucky Doris Jackson That's the way she always acted when she was in the store.

One night after work I asked her to have dinner at my apartment, which was above the store then. I made my specialty *coq au vin,* except it was with chicken, and we finished off a bottle of wine and I played her my Mozart records and we drank a couple of cognacs. She was wearing a pretty blue dress with white cuffs and a long white collar and her hair was back in a bun. Even back then, she looked tired around the eyes, but she had a bright smile on her face. She looked like a happy, hard-working, sort-of vulnerable, really attractive woman who been through more than most. She asked what I was waiting for, and I took her to my bed.

She spent some nights after that in my apartment. We were warm with each other and gentle, but sometimes I was rough too, and she cried, but I don't think because I was hurting her, and the tears were happy tears too. I think we both needed that sort-of rough stuff. But we always fell asleep with our arms around each other.

Then her sonovabitch husband came to the island. He found out where she worked and one morning he was drunk and he met her in front of the store and she stumbled in with a puffy cheek, a cut lip and a swollen eye. I was gonna call the police but she begged me not to, saying it was her fault, she was a married woman who had slept with other men.

I ran outside, he was still there, and I started yelling at him and he pushed me to the ground. I got up and started wrestling with him, he was over six feet with plenty of muscles. He got me in a headlock and was twisting. I raised my free arm to try to punch him and he saw the numbers, I always wear short-sleeve shirts. Then he said: "What the fuck? *Goddamn*, man!"

He let go of my head and stumbled off down the street, shaking his head. That was my one and only meeting with John Jackson.

Doris stayed at my apartment for a couple of weeks until she found a new place. Over the years, he's made other trips to the island and always found her. The last time I saw them together, they were walking down Calle Cristo, going into a restaurant. They were holding hands. Sometimes you just got to scratch your head and pity people. Which was what Doris Jackson was probably doing now, concerning me.

EIGHTEEN

"Excuse me, do you speak English?"

Stevie nodded.

I'm sorry to bother you, but I'm having a little trouble reading this map. I'm looking for Calle Las Monjas. I see here a Caleta de las Monjas, and I am wondering if it's the same and . . ."

She had these soft brown eyes. Her metal-rimmed sunglasses were pushed to the top of her head. Her dark brown hair was pulled back into a ponytail. Her lips were full, very full. She had a nice, slightly curved jaw. Her skin was tanned. Stevie closed his notebook. He tapped the space next to him. She didn't seem to be wearing any face makeup. She wore dangling silver earrings. Her short-sleeved top was striped blue and white. Her blue skirt was tight enough to accent attractive curves. Lovely legs, Blue slip-on boat shoes. A brown leather bag slung over her. *Thank you, God, for making this my day off and sending me to sit and write on my usual bench in Plaza San José.*

She showed him the map and a sheet of paper she took out of her bag with an address written on it.

"I'll take you there," he said,

"No, no, you don't have to," she said.

"It's O.K. I was just going in that direction myself."

She gave him a suspicious look. He smiled. She smiled.

"O.K.," she said. "That's very nice of you. Thanks."

They introduced themselves—Stevie Díaz. Sharon Peterson—then headed down Calle Cristo, passed the San Juan Cathedral—home of the remains, said Stevie, of Ponce de León—then turned toward El Convento Hotel, the former home, noted Stevie, of nuns.

Sharon nodded.

Was she here as a tourist?

"Sort of," she said. No further explanation.

Where was she from?

"Ohio. Youngstown, Ohio."

Where was she staying?

"At a guest house. It's just a couple of blocks down from the plaza where I asked you for directions."

They went down Caleta de las Monjas. They found the address: a two-story, restored, light green-colored house with wooden balconies. Sharon again thanked Stevie, "If you want, I could wait and if you want, we could . . ."

"Oh, no, that won't be necessary. You're very nice." She smiled. She gave him a little wave. She turned and rang the front doorbell.

Stevie walked back up to the top of the street and sat on a bench in front of El Convento. She almost certainly would have to pass this way. He'd give her fifteen, twenty minutes.

Just a few minutes later, she was trudging back up the street. There were tears in her eyes.

Stevie jumped up from the bench. "What's wrong?"

"She's not there. My Mom's not there, Oh, Jesus!" She searched in her bag, couldn't find a hankie or Kleenex.

Stevie pulled from the back pocket of his khakis a blue paisley bandana he used as a handkerchief. "Here, take this. It's clean."

Sharon took the bandana, wiped her eyes, blew her nose. "Oh, thanks." She offered it back.

"Keep it," Stevie said. "I got lots of them. And come with me for a beer or something."

She nodded and Stevie led her into El Convento, through the lobby and out into the patio. The sat at a table beneath a huge shady tree, which Stevie knew was a *nispero* fruit tree from Spain. (He remembered looking it up when he first saw it.)

Sharon said she would like a beer and Stevie ordered two *Coronas*. The waiter poured the beer from the bottles, tipping the glasses to produce a generous froth. They smiled their thanks, sipped. A tiny foam mustache formed on Sharon's upper lip. She licked it away, then told Stevie her story.

"My Mom, Lydia Ortiz, is from Puerto Rico. She was a nurse at a hospital in San Juan before she was recruited by a hospital in Cleveland looking for Spanish speaking nurses. So she went up to Cleveland and she met and married William Peterson, my Dad, and they moved to Youngstown. He's sort of a doctor, a chiropractor.

And a sonovabitch. They never got along, he was always berating her. So three years ago, when I started at Ohio University, they split. Then they got back together last year. Then. a couple of months ago, my Mom left him again and this time she came home. To Puerto Rico. She called me at school and we cried and she gave me her address where she would be staying. I told her, 'please don't leave me,' and she said, she wasn't leaving me, she was leaving the sonovabitch, and when I graduate, which is next year if I want I can come to live with her. Here, in Puerto Rico. My Mom was a bit of a bohemian. She told me that when she was at the University she hung out with the writers and the painters in Old San Juan. I suppose that's why she came back to the Old City. So we have a week break and I came down here—to find Mom. The address she gave me, she isn't there anymore, the woman who owns the house and rented the room said. Mom moved out a couple of weeks ago and the woman doesn't know where, or why."

Did the woman say anything at all about your mother, where she might have gone?"

"Only that Mom moved. Nothing more. So now what do I do?"

"What *we* do," said Stevie, "is continue to look for your mother."

"How?"

"Do you have a photo of her, a recent one?"

Sharon went into her bag and slid out of a wallet pocket a picture of her mom, Lydia Ortiz, an attractive looking woman with lots of black curly hair who didn't look older than forty.

"We'll show the photo in the stores, restaurants and . . . um, bars. The Old City is just small enough. If she was here for some months, she may be recognized by someone who knows her, knows a friend, or something."

Sharon frowned. "That sounds . . . rather desperate."

Stevie shrugged. "It's worth a try. Coincidences are always happening here. People know people who are related and have friends and . . ."

Sharon forced a smile onto her lovely lips. "O.K," she said.

First stop was back up the hill to El Patio de Sam, the hangout for poets, painters, politicos, and others. Neither Perry, the bartender nor Jorgito, the manager, recognized the photo. Stevie led Sharon around to several other Old City's restaurants—showing the photo to the serious-faced, middle-aged waiters at La Bombonera, to the staffs at La Mallorca, La Mallorquina, Barrachina, La Fonda Del Callejon, Amadeus, El Siglo XX, Amanda's and a half dozen more.

Unfortunately, *nada.*

Stevie invited Sharon to dinner at Amanda's, which was just a few buildings down from his apartment. They sat at a table outside and ate tacos and watched the sunset sky glow from orange to purple.

After dinner, they did the many bars around town, mostly those where the expatriates—gay, straight and whatever else—would spend time: the One World. Corbett's, Blanche's Place, El Batey. the Malomundo.

Dickie Dubois, who owned and bartended at Blanche's Place, took the photo under a light, blinked his long, false eyelashes and shook his dyed blond head. "No, no, no straight woman this classy-looking would dare step into this place," he said sadly.

Ernesto, El Batey's tall, muscular, eye-patched, tattoo-armed bartender who looked like a fun-loving pirate, gave Stevie and Sharon the easy, wide, space-toothed smile he gave all customers not to scare them away. His good eye focused in on the photo. "Sorry," he said, shaking his head like the woman in the photo represented a missed opportunity. "If she was here at any time I *sure* would have noticed her, and talked about many things with her," Norman, the pirate lookalike, said.

Several beers later, the searchers lucked out—at Malomundo, with Fritzie the German bartender.

"Ya, ya," said Fritzie, rubbing her chin. "Such a nice woman, she would come in here always wit' dat painter, Paco . . . you know, he's dat famous painter. Paco."

"Do you know where we could find the painter?" Stevie asked.

"He comes in here from time to time. "If you want, give me your name and contact and when he comes in . . ."

"Do you know if he lives in Old San Juan?"

Some guy at the bar wearing khaki shorts and shirt and a pith helmet who overheard the conversation said with a British accent: "I say, old chap, are you looking for Paco Soto, the artist?"

Stevie nodded.

The guy patted down his long gray twitching mustache and said: "He teaches courses over at the School of Fine Arts at El Morro, the former Spanish fortress grounds turned U.S. Army base then given over to the commonwealth government which allows it to be swarmed over by tourists and all the locals. If you find the sonovabitch, tell him he still owes me many quid for the drinks I keep buying him and the other bloody Wogs. I'm called El Gringo

Loco, though, of course, I was once a Brigadier—you know, with a crown and three pips—in Her Majesty's Service."

Stevie nodded, took Sharon's hand. "Yeah, sure," They left the bar.

It was too late to go to the art school so they returned to Sam's Patio and had a few more beers, Stevie told Sharon that while the sunset sky was beautiful, she should *really* see the sky over the ocean at sunrise, which could be viewed from the balcony of his apartment and Sharon agreed to spend the night there if Stevie promised they would arise early enough to see the sunrise sky. Stevie said, yes, they would rise with the sun.

As they walked back along Boulevard del Valle to Stevie's house, Sharon held tight to Stevie's arm. "I'm a little woozy," she said.

They reached the four-story yellow brick building. "I live on the top floor," Stevie said.

"I hope I can make it," Sharon said.

She did and as soon as they got inside the apartment, she fell fast into Stevie's arms and they kissed, sweetly. Stevie led her into the bedroom and turned on the overhead wooden fan and they slid onto Stevie's narrow bed and their tongues touched and then he stood, and she did also, and, wobbling a little, they both took off their clothes and got onto the cool sheets, hugging, kissing, and Stevie slid inside her.

Sharon told Stevie he was really a good guy, gentle and sincere and honest. What did he plan to do with his life?

Stevie told her he was writing a novel. That was the first step.

Sharon then confessed that she too wanted to be a writer. She had had two short stories published in a little magazine in Ohio.

"Really?" Stevie said. "That's *great!* What are the stories about?"

"Well, they're both about a young woman who wants, well, to be a writer, and to be a lover, and to find something real and permanent in her life, but who knows if she achieves the first two—writer and lover—she can never reach the third."

Stevie put a hand over his mouth. He looked at Sharon with a sort of painful expression. Then he put out his hands palms up. "Why?"

"Because writing and loving take up all the time and space and don't fit into the workings of the real world.

Stevie nodded. Shrugged. "I see. Sort of."

They made love again, then fell asleep in each other's arms.

They missed the sunrise sky.

NINETEEN

I went into the hallway of my house and was about to go up to my apartment when I fell over something at the bottom of the stairs. The hallway lights weren't working as usual. It stirred and made a little groaning sound.

It was Carmen. She looked almost dead, but she was alive.

"Hello, Papi," she said. "I lost the key you give me. So I been waitin' for you."

Even in the dark, I could see she was sick. Her face was glistening sweat and her eyes were huge and bulging.

"I got to talk wit' you," she said.

"So talk."

"I been sick the last few days, you know? Manny give me drugs, but now he don' wanna give me no more. I seen him a couple of hours ago. I asked him to put me straight, you know? But he said no more free shit and he wasn't goin' to open no credit account for me, I told him I been sick but he say that don't matter, I should borrow money or steal it. He said I'm into him for too much money already. That mossafucker, he know I always pay him. So that's why I'm here, Papi. I need forty dollar."

I just looked at her. I was more sad than angry.

She said: "I'm sorry, Papi · But I ain't got no place else to go for the money, you know?"

"Come on upstairs and I'll get you the money," I told her.

Carmen couldn't get up. I helped her to her feet. Then she bent over like she was a jack-knife trying to close. "Ai-ai-ai-ai-ai," she cried.

I picked her up and carried her up the stairs. She didn't weigh no more than my Rachel. I felt I was carrying someone who was dying.

I put Carmen down to get the key. She held tight onto my arm. I opened the door and helped her in, then put her into my leather armchair, then switched on the lights. She looked terrible. Her face was covered with sweat and it was gray and her mouth was twitching, it was twisted to one side.

I went to the kitchen and got her a glass of water. She drank about half of it; then it came up through her nose and mouth. She bent over in the chair and made vomiting sounds, but nothing came up. Then she slipped off the chair onto the floor and curled up like she was in a womb.

I kneeled down next to her, picked her up and put her on the couch. She was shivering and I went to the closet and got my raincoat and covered her with it.

"I gotta have some dope," She was crying. "Manny say he gonna be back in the restaurant on Calle Luna at ten o'clock. Can you go there for me? I can't go nowhere. Tell Manny he should give you four dime bags. Ai-ai- ai-ai-ai!"

"You've got to give it up again," I said. "You stay here and I'll take care of you. Like the last time."

"Yeah, but no. Not now. I'm sorry, baby. I'm so sick. I can't do it now. I got to have dope or I'm gonna die! Please, Papi, please! Get me the dope. I am so sick."

I wanted to kick her out but I wanted more for her to stay, don't ask me why.

One more chance. No more!

I went to the dresser in the bedroom and took out some money from a shirt pocket. I looked at my watch. It was nine-thirty. I went over to the couch. Carmen was still shaking and there was sweat all over her face. "I'll be back soon as I can," I told her.

She tried to smile, but couldn't make it. *"Gracias*, Papi."

I had three cups of coffee and it was past eleven and that sonovabitch still didn't show up. Sitting across from me and cackling were some guys in women's clothes. They had on heavy makeup and some of them had the beginning of breasts, which were swelling over their low-cut dresses. I went over to their table.

"You know where I can find Manny?" I asked them.

They all got quiet and looked at me like I just came off another planet.

"I'm looking for Manny," I said.

A pretty little thing with blond hair over one eye, you could swear it was a girl if you didn't see the big Adam's apple and the black hairs on the hands above the knuckles, said, "I seen him about fifteen minutes ago, he was going into the Paradise Club."

I went down the block to the Paradise Club, a hangout for homosexuals. I was a few yards away when I seen Manny coming out of the club. He began walking towards the corner, away from the restaurant. I went after him.

Manny was passing darkened stores and the soles on his shoes were slapping against the sidewalk. The street was deserted.

Then, just as he got to the corner and I was going to call him, a long dark car came speeding down the street. Its brakes screeched, the front door flew open and two guys jumped out. One of them grabbed Manny's arm and twisted it up his back. The other was Hector, the gorilla who was in the restaurant the other night, and he punched Manny hard in the stomach. Manny doubled over and held his stomach with his free hand and his body jerked forward. The guy holding his arm thought Manny was trying to break away so he twisted the arm some more and you could hear something crack. I yelled out, but Hector and his friend didn't look up. They were too busy ripping Manny's sports jacket off and taking a wallet from the inside pocket and taking out the money inside the wallet and throwing the wallet on the ground and going through his other pockets and taking a bunch of small envelopes from the jacket and from Manny's pants pocket a gun which Hector put in his own pocket.

Then Manny straightened up and looked like he was going to fall backward. But what he did was bring his left knee up hard. But it missed Hector's groin and then a knife was in Hector's hand. The knife disappeared into Manny's shoulder, then came out again. Hector wiped it off on Manny's shirt and put it back in his pocket. I was yelling some more and Hector looked over to me. He was breathing heavy, but he gave me a space-toothed grin. "Manny did a double-cross," Hector told me. "You shouldn't trust him."

Then he and the other guy were back in the car which went squealing in reverse back up the street, then sped off around a corner.

I went to Manny. The upper part of his shirt was soaked dark with blood and his arm was hanging crooked at his side. His face was as white as the part of his shirt that wasn't bloody. He was gasping for breath and his eyelids were fluttering. Then he opened his eyes and seen me.

"Help me, Wolf," he said. "Get a taxi and take me to the hospital. Please!"

"O.K.," I told him. "I'll put you in a taxi. But first, you got to give me four dime bags for Carmen." Then I added: "I got the money to pay you for them."

He did something with his mouth and I thought he was going to grin, but then it started twitching and he closed his eyes and bit his lip. "Aw, fuck," he said. "I'm dying, you asshole! Get me to the fuckin' hospital!"

I looked down at him. I wanted to leave that sonovabitch right there to die on the street. When he looked at me again, there was pleading in his eyes.

"Those motherfuckers ripped off everything I had," he said. "After they fix me up at the hospital I'll get you some horse. I promise."

I picked up Manny's sports jacket from the ground. I turned it inside out and bunched it up and put it over the wound to stop the bleeding.

"Hey, man," Manny said, "That's a two-hundred-fifty-dollar jacket!"

"Would you rather bleed to death?"

He grunted and I told him to hold the jacket there. I ran two blocks to the Plaza Colon and got a cab. There were five or six people standing around Manny when we pulled up. The driver helped me put Manny in the back seat and I told him to take us to Presbyterian Hospital. On our way there, Manny said: "I'm gonna say I was mugged and when I fought back I got knifed, and I'm gonna say I don't know who did it. I got my own way of getting back at those *cabrónes,* they gonna be *dead!* And I'm gonna say you came along and found me and I don't know you from shit, dig Wolf?"

"Yeah," I told him. I wondered how Carmen was holding out.

By the time Manny got treated and we left the hospital—I had to write a check for two hundred seventy-eight dollars for the treatment—it was three in the morning. Besides the knife wound, a bone in his left shoulder was broken. We got another taxi and took it to Bayamón. The cab waited while I went with Manny to his house and he gave me four of those little glassine envelopes and said, "No charge, Wolf. We're even from what you laid out at the hospital.

What are you talking about?" I said.

"Excuse me now, I got to check on my kid," he said and disappeared into a back room.

I had a great urge to run after him and break his other arm. But I got nervous thinking about Carmen, and I ran outside and took the taxi back to my apartment.

I opened the door and almost walked into Carmen. She was right by the door, bent over and contorted, her arms squeezing her body like it was about to fall apart. She had put the lights out and all I could see of her face were two huge dark caverns with little trapped animals inside, which were her eyes. She was shivering and I could hear her teeth chattering.

I switched on the light. She shut her eyes and made a little whelp like the sound a dog sometimes makes in its sleep. I gave her the envelopes and she grunted something and started to leave, but then she turned and her face was all pain and she said, "Papi, can I shoot up here? I sorry, but I can't make it nowhere else."

"Yeah," I said. "O.K., go ahead."

She did what she had to do in front of me, with the matches and the bottle cap and the needle and everything.

She didn't shoot it in her arm but in the back of her hand. Just before she put the needle in, she took off the crucifix from around her neck and looked up at me and gave me a real shaky smile like I was watching her do the most shameful thing there was.

After a few minutes, she began to relax. I was sitting in my leather armchair and she sat cross-legged on the floor in front of me. "*Ay*, Papi, you the best person I know," she said.

I didn't say nothing. I looked down at her eyes. They were shiny and black and there was a glazed happiness in them, and I started to relax like Carmen's heroin was working on me too.

"I feel so-o-o good now, baby," Carmen said.

"How you gonna feel tomorrow?" I asked her.

She smiled lazily. "I wanna stay wit' you, Papi. Give me another chance, O.K.?"

"Why'd you leave the last time?"

"I got a message that Manny wanted to talk to me about a family t'ing."

"Was that what that kid told you that night in the plaza?"

She nodded.

"You should of told me," I said.

"Yeah, baby, but like, I wanted to see Manny, you know? Maybe he was gonna tell me somet'ing about my sister," Carmen said.

I grunted.

Carmen's lids were starting to close. She pulled her head up and snapped open her eyes like she just been surprised. "Manny says to me he's losin' money because I ain't buyin' the dope from him no more, you know? He's real pissed off, you know? He said I was takin' milk from his baby. I tol' him he should fuck himself in the *culo* and he laughed real loud and said he was only kiddin', he got a present for me. And he gimme some bags, you know, he said it's for free. So I took them and went down to my house in La Perla and I split the dope with my brother. And Manny come over there every day and keep giving it free because, he said, we was family. Until a couple of days ago, he says he wants the money, I should go out and get some 'cause he ain't giving no more shit away for nothin' So that's why I here, Papi."

"Why'd you start taking that crap again?" I could have smacked her, I was so mad. She was weaker than I wanted her to be.

"I dunno," Carmen said. "I was feelin' nervous, you know?"

"What d'ya mean?"

"I dunno. You was gonna take me to all those places in New York, it made me nervous."

"You been there before, what are you talking about?"

"Yeah, but, you know. You was gonna take me to places I ain't been before."

"Didn't you want to go? If you didn't, why didn't you say something?"

"I wanted to go. But like, I got nervous, you know?"

I looked deep at Carmen. She gave me a little sleepy smile again. Her eyes closed and she started nodding off.

This time, we'd go slower. I was going to get her off drugs again. And if I had to shoot Manny dead to make sure that happened, I would do it. Gladly.

I fell asleep in the chair. When I woke, Carmen was on the floor crunched up again like a fetus in a crooked womb. She was sucking her thumb. I picked her up and carried her into the bedroom and put her on the bed and she opened her eyes, farted, smiled, closed her eyes and got into the same twisted-up position.

The next day I went to see Julia and gave her money for a week at her place in Boquerón again.

We went out there again and Carmen came out of hell again.

When we got back to San Juan, I bought more art materials and started on another painting of her. She cleaned the house from top to bottom and got down on her hands and knees to scrub the floors. She picked up the book on Leonardo da Vinci and this time looked like she got real interested in it.

"How did he do all this so long ago, Papi?" she asked me.

"He showed what a human being could do, at any time, besides all the shit they been doing. People got it in them to do all sorts of things," I said.

"¡*Que bueno!*" Carmen said.

The next morning, me and Slatsky seen each other on the street. He invited me into La Bombonera for a cup of coffee and we made up. Which is something we both wanted to do.

We both been through too much of the same things to let that night with his schmuck brother-in-law keep us from being friends. He asked me to dinner again and I said I was bringing Carmen and he said he wasn't going to invite his brother-in-law.

We had a wonderful time. Olga made a delicious fish escabeche. We drank a couple bottles of Spanish wine. Olga played some old records by Vincentico Valdez and Olga Guillot and Daniel Santos and Carmen and Olga knew all the words and they sang along with the records and made me and Slatsky get up and dance with them.

Olga was full of fun and for the first time, I seen Carmen really become animated too. Slatsky's twins, Richie and Tommy, came out of the bedroom, saying the music woke them up. Carmen gave them milk and cookies and we had coffee and cake and as I looked at everyone sitting around the big kitchen table, I got this feeling inside—it was a soft, warm pain. I seen the possibilities. What kind of life me and Carmen could have had with each other—if we were completely different people. Which we weren't.

Then, when we got home, we were going to make love, only I couldn't. Which was the first time I couldn't get a hard-on with Carmen. She curled up against my side and said over and over: "I love you, I love you."

For the first time since I met Carmen, since she put life and feeling back into me, I felt what I was going to be very soon. An old old man. But I felt something else too, it wasn't so bad. It was something more peaceful.

I seen another possibility. Of our life together now as we were. A reformed junkie who could be shooting up again tomorrow, and an old crab who thinks people should be better than they are but they ain't, and he ain't too. Maybe I couldn't get no hard-on because I was having these "soft" thoughts. But it didn't bother me. It even made me feel good, that I seen the . . . possibilities. Even for us.

The next few days we were closer than we ever been. Something was shining in Carmen's eyes that wasn't there before, a hard, clear light. I went to the store only a couple of hours each day, letting Don Alfonso take care of going in and out of the safe, he knew the combination. Carmen and me took long walks around Old San Juan and along the waterfront. We went to the beach and I taught Carmen to swim. Which I never could before, but now she made up her mind she would learn, no matter what. Carmen spent a lot of time mending my books that were cut up during the break-in. She worked on them hours at a time, sitting on the cracked tile floor, the books all around her, her legs crossed, her back straight, her head bent, her hair covering the sides of her face, scotch taping pages and gluing bindings like she was putting back together more than the books.

She wanted me to teach her better English. She bought a notebook and spent lots of time looking into the big Velazquez Spanish-English dictionary I bought her and printing very slow in the notebook and asking me how to say the words, which she learned to pronounce with a Spanish-Polish accent.

Carmen found a way to fight the urge for drugs. She went to church every day. She said "Papa Dios" heard her prayers and took away the feeling that she needed drugs. Whatever took it away was O.K. with me and I went with her to the San Francisco Church and sat in back and stared at the painted wooden saints in the niches of the white-washed walls while people were sitting on the benches and kneeling in front of them and Carmen was up front at the railing, kneeling and praying and crossing herself and looking up with big eyes at the head-hanging crucified Christ over the altar, and doing whatever else it takes to get his attention. The priest there, Father Venard, he was always dressed in a monk's robe, would always say hello to me and Carmen. He helped the poor in La Perla and he helped the addicts get off the drugs, so sometimes religion ain't so bad, it can do good things.

We made plans again to go up to New York, and this time she said she was really looking forward to it, and I think she was. I asked her what she wanted to do more than anything there and she said she wanted to go walking with me in Central Park. "All the years I been up there, I only been to the park to buy drugs," she said.

I said we could go ice skating on the lake and she was surprised that there was a lake in the park. "I wanna do that," she said. "I wanna learn to skate on the ice."

We went to a couple of department stores to buy what warm clothes for her we could find. Carmen especially wanted a fur hat, which we would have to wait till we got to New York to buy. I got her a coat with a fur collar which she loved and some gloves and a nice wool scarf.

"I don't know much from life, except things like doing drugs and bein' a whore," Carmen said one night in bed. "But I want you should show me other things, Papi. It ain't too late, is it?" Her black eyes stared up at me with a look that I shouldn't hurt her, which she knew I wasn't going to, but she put it there to make sure I didn't.

I said, "No, it ain't too late. As long as you're alive, it ain't too late."

That night we went for a walk and wound up sitting on a bench in Plaza San José, where there's a statue of Ponce de *León* and the San José Church. On one side of the plaza is the museum of Pablo Casals, the Spanish cellist, he lived on the island for many years he was in exile from the Franco government. I told Carmen he played so wonderful it could bring tears to your eyes.

Carmen looked at me with her sleepy smile. "Sometimes you see or hear something so beautiful you got to cry, right Papi? It makes you feel those things deep down and they make it worth why you are living. I don't say it right, but you know what I mean."

I grunted.

We started to walk back home, along Calle San Sebastian. Young guys with frowning mustaches were sitting on car fenders and standing in front of old, flaking buildings that had slogans painted on them like "Yankee Go Home" and "Puerto Rico Libre" and some of them gave me a look like it was only me that stood in the way of justice for Puerto Rico. Latin music was blaring out into the street from jukeboxes in the bars and sort-of nightclubs and crushed beer cans were doubled over along the curb and there was the smell of marijuana and of warm bread from a nearby bakery.

We passed a Pentecostal church. It was jumping with tambourines and trumpets playing and people singing with the music coming into the streets from the open doors. The blue bricks on the streets were shining under the lampposts. We came to the wall where all the misfits hang out. A guy with a voice that sounded like it was scraped with a razor asked me for a quarter. When I gave it to him he said, "Thanks friend," and then he said, "Times is hard." I nodded and he got angry. "How the hell would you know?" he said. I just looked at him and he broke into a grin and winked.

We walked down to Plaza Colón. The buses were fuming and farting and spewing out people. A group of kids were standing in the plaza with bibles. They looked like they just came out of the dry-cleaning machine along with their clothes. They were preaching and singing about Jesus through loudspeakers turned up to wake the dead, while guys standing on the corner were pursing their lips and making kissing sounds at girls passing by in tight pants. It was a real Saturday night in Old San Juan.

I got a lot of bitterness inside me. Still, just then, I was thinking this ain't a bad place to live. Over the years I've gotten to like it. I almost felt at home in the world.

TWENTY

Doris, walking to the store from her apartment, got this strange feeling. Not exactly that she was being followed, but more like . . . something, it made her nervous as hell.

Her premonition came true. There he was, leaning against the storefront window, a white gleaming smile. Some of the teeth in the top row, she remembered, were part of a bridge (The real ones were knocked out in a motorcycle accident on the FDR Drive just after he graduated from law school.)

She looked at her watch. It was 9:05. She looked up. His face was more creased than ever. Like he hadn't slept all night. Which she was sure he hadn't. Every part of her weakened.

Oh, shit! Was history actually about to repeat itself? What the fuck could she do? Run, hide, rush into the store, shout for the police?

"*Hello* darling. I went to the club again and they told me you only sing on the weekends. So I figured that along with the singing gig you still have your old job, which I see that you do, which makes me very happy now, dearest because after an all-nighter in the wonderful bars of the Old City I have once again found you, and once more, we can renew the love of both of our lives."

Doris shut her eyes. He didn't go away. His eyes were as glassy as she had ever seen them. His arms hung loosely from the rolled-up sleeves of a black tee shirt with "Life Is a Beach" white lettering on it.

Sweat was beginning to dampen Doris' body beneath her new white satiny blouse and light blue slacks.

"Look, *I told* you. I'm not going to see you . . ."

"Oh, come on, sweetheart. You know that you miss me as much as I miss you, that only I can find that spot that sends you flying over the moon. You know that it's only us that matter." He grabbed her by the arms and tried to kiss her.

"Let me go!" Doris shouted, looking around. A few passersby took in the scene and went on.

He pushed her arms up her back and pulled her tight against him. The bad breath-alcohol smell was coming out of the pores of his face.

Why the hell wasn't she carrying mace, pepper spray, a goddamn pistol like a lot of other women were starting to do?

"I love you, darling. You know, that's what's deepest inside you too. You *know* that only you and me . . ."

"*Goddamnit, let me go!*"

He looked deep into her eyes. Then his face lit up and he smiled. He knew she was kidding. "I love you," he said again.

Doris stared back at him. "Your *love* means nothing to me anymore. Because coming from you, it is just a word. That word only means something if you have empathized, sympathized, humanized your supposed feelings. I'm not going to wait around to see if you have learned that." She said it all calmly, surprising herself.

John Jackson gave Doris a befuddled look. Then he actually let her go.

Her eyes filled with tears.

"I'm sorry," he said. "Just let me . . ."

"Look, it's over. It's over."

"I'm sorry." John Jackson said again. There were tears in his eyes also. "I've had a relapse. I see that I cannot mix my medications with my senseless boozing. Forgive me, Doris—forgive me Doctor Maria Wellington of the New York-Presbyterian Hospital. I'm not going to bother Doris anymore."

Doris watched him weave, then stumble down the street. She shook her head, wiped her eyes, mascara blotting her hankie, then tucked her blouse into her slacks and went into the store. Wolf was straightening out jewelry under a counter.

Doris greeted him and he looked up at her, then smiled and winked. "Good morning, my dear. How you doing?"

"I'm fine. How are *you* doing?

"Not too bad," Wolf said.

"I'll be right back," she said, heading for the bathroom in the back.

She removed the remaining mascara from under her eyes and washed her face, then blotted it dry with a paper towel. She looked fairly decent. Then she wondered whether people could actually change. Could this lousy world actually get better—for me and for others?

Who would have thunk it?

TWENTY-ONE

A couple of nights later, I took Carmen to El Patio de Sam for dinner. It was a Friday night and the place was packed and we couldn't find an empty table. We were about to leave for another restaurant when Larry Cruz, the artist who I meet from time to time by accident and we usually have a cup of coffee together, he came up to us and asked if we wanted to join him and his wife at their table, there were two empty chairs there.

Larry introduced his wife, Betty, and I introduced Carmen. We sat smiling. I store-signaled the waiter. Carmen ordered chicken and *mofongo,* which is fried plantains with lots of garlic, and I ordered a hamburger. I had a Corona beer and Carmen drank a Coke. Betty leaned over the table toward Carmen and asked her: "Do you work at Mr. Wolf's store?

"No, I ain't been working," Carmen said. "I was takin' drugs."

Larry and Betty gave each other looks, between *"what?"* and "well . . ."

Carmen said: "I gave 'em up. I don't take them no more."

"That's great!" said Betty.

Betty and Carmen talked about Brooklyn, where they both once lived, and Betty said she quit her job teaching English at a private school there, she wanted to teach Puerto Rican kids on the island, and she and Larry moved back to where they were both born, and soon Betty and Carmen were laughing about something, I didn't catch it. They kept talking and I heard Betty tell Carmen: "You know, you may have dropped out of school, but you learned from life what lots of people, even with college degrees, never learn, or understand,"

Betty squeezed Carmen's hand and Carmen smiled.

So we were talking and joking and having a good time and Larry insisted on buying us glasses of cognac and we left the restaurant after midnight. Before we parted, Betty invited Carmen and me for dinner at their house on Sunday.

They lived on top of the Old City, in an apartment on the top floor. Larry's posters and prints were all over the walls of their apartment, telling about government-sponsored events for the Institute of Puerto Rican Culture and there were others which he said were from his days in Vietnam, but there were no pictures of soldiers fighting or airplanes bombing, but instead they showed old people with scary creased faces and little kids with frightened faces and Vietnamese women, most of them beautiful. We went up some metal stairs in the hallway to the wide roof of the building that overlooked the ocean and where we sat on straw rockers and drank *mojitos* and watched the sun, huge, a crimson color, slide down behind the line between the sea and the sky. Carmen and Lucy, the 10-year-old daughter of Larry and Betty, sat on a large straw mat out there, playing card games and laughing. Larry, Betty and me, we talked about lots of things. Larry asked me about what Poland and Lithuania was like when I lived there, and I told them some funny stories when I was a kid, including how I used to get in trouble at school starting fights with blackboard erasers, and then we went on to other things, about wars and how some people treated other people, and I saw tears starting in Betty's eyes, so I stopped with those stories.

Then Betty went downstairs into the kitchen and Carmen got up from the mat and went there also and soon they brought up some delicious *carne guisada,* which is a simple beef stew with rice and olives and lots of good seasoning. Betty was really nice with Carmen, telling her that she and her daughter want to see her again. "You too, Mr. Wolf," she said, and everyone laughed.

The next Friday they came to my apartment and I bought some new dishes and Carmen helped me cook *coq au vin* and we had plenty of wine to drink. We listened to Mozart records and Carmen played salsa music from the radio and Larry and Betty danced and Carmen made me dance with her, and we switched partners and little Lucy was also dancing, everyone was having a great time.

In the next weeks me and Larry had lunch together at the Mallorquina restaurant a couple of times and Betty and Lucy and Carmen went together for lunch also, then they went to *Parque de las Palomas,* which is the Pigeon's Park, were hundreds and hundreds of pigeons live and they got the pigeons to come out of their homes which were holes made in the side of a concrete wall next to the park by feeding them peanuts they bought from the wagon that was at the gate. Carmen baby-sat some nights when Larry and Betty went to a movie and Betty told Carmen she was really smart and should try to get a high school diploma, and she even gave Carmen some books and came to the house so they could read the books together and she would help Carmen learn the lessons and kept telling her she was smarter than she thought and could get a good job if she wanted one.

We met again at El Patio de Sam for dinner and drinks.

So things were going O.K. again.

But I wasn't doing no somersaults.

TWENTY-TWO

They woke at noon, smiling at each other at the same time. Neither said anything about missing the sunrise sky.

"I'll make us breakfast, lunch, brunch, whatever," said Stevie. "We can eat out on the balcony."

Stevie got out of bed, looking down at Sharon, who blinked her eyes several times. "*Chévere,*" she said. "See, I'm already going native."

"Hey, native," said Stevie, "I'm gonna give you a good-morning kiss. Get up here."

"You get back down here," Sharon said. "You're in my country now."

"O.K.," said Stevie, "But it's my country too."

He got back in bed and, side-by-side, he began kissing her neck and ear. Sharon giggled. They licked. They kissed, deeply, around their unbrushed teeth, So what? Down she went, until he told her "O.K." and then he wiggled his tongue inside her; then he raised himself and maneuvered her beneath him, and slid inside, and she gripped his neck with her suddenly powerful arms and Sharon and Stevie twisted and rocked and then they both moaned and trembled as the morning-afternoon got off to a *really* rousing start.

Stevie made coffee in his Mr. Coffee maker. He served the steaming black liquid with *pan de agua* browned in his small toaster, butter in a dish, a plate of leftover *chorizo* and large slices of *brazo gitano* he still had in his small fridge. He instructed Sharon that the "gypsy's arm" she would be eating was actually guava paste and cheese rolled into a sponge cake. Sharon passed on the *chorizo* but loved the cake and Stevie gave her half his. They ate and they drank strong black Puerto Rican mountain-grown coffee with a couple spoonfuls of sugar. A few small, puffy, white clouds cotton-balled the sky and blocked out the sun from time to time and they sat with their white coffee mugs in their hands and watched the ocean going from blue to green to shiny blue-green.

Stevie stood, kissed Karen on the cheek and told her they should go over to the School of Fine Arts to find Paco Soto and ask him if he knew the whereabouts of Sharon's mom.

They walked the five or six blocks along Calle Norzagaray to El Morro. The School of Fine Arts was on the grounds of the old fortress. Very few people and practically no students were in the workshops or the offices. Stevie and Sharon were told by a security guard that the students and instructors were on a between-semesters break.

"Hey," said a sort-of surprised Sharon, "just like me." Then she asked Stevie: "Now what?"

"We go back to bed," Stevie said.

Which they did.

Sharon checked out of her guesthouse and moved in with Stevie for the few days she had left before returning to school in Ohio. They took turns cooking in the crumby little kitchenette and they ate out on Stevie's payday and the day after, and they couldn't wait to tumble into bed, day or night. They never saw a sunrise, but they did see sunset skies and Stevie read to Sharon the first chapters of his novel and she was, well, somewhat enthused, telling him he was a wonderful writer, but she wished he was writing about his life. Stevie said the book *was* about his life, only projected on a character at a different time in another place.

"O.K.," Sharon said, "I see. Sort of."

One evening, after one hour and three beers at the bar of Sam's Patio, Perry, the bartender, introduced them to Carlos Ferrer, the painter, who specialized in portraits. His subjects were either wealthy families or street people, the latter who he invited into his studio with food and drink. Ferrer said he was a close friend of Paco Soto, "even though—don't ever tell him—his color fields leave me cold." He smiled warmly, giving a clue that he was kidding, sort of, and that the two artists often chided one another for their styles and subjects, but not without a grudging admiration each had for the other. The artist was shown the photo of Sharon's mom.

"She's a good friend of Soto's," Stevie said. "Do you know her?"

Ferrer looked at the photo, sort of nodded. "Yeah, she looks familiar. But, you know, who can keep up with Paco and his women?"

Sharon gave Stevie a hurt look, and Stevie said, "Do you know where we could find Paco Soto now?"

Ferrer knew Soto was very close to his son and daughter and his grandchildren, all of whom he usually visited when he got a break from the school, where both artists taught. Stevie got a sudden vision of taking Sharon to meet the artist, who just may have taken her mom out there to meet the family. They would all get together in lovely casitas out on the island, in the rolling green hills and the cool air of the Cordillera Central.

"Do you know where the family lives?" Stevie asked.

"Sí," said Carlos Ferrer. "In a coincidence, his family lives in the town where I once worked. Bayonne."

"Bayonne? That's in what part of the island?" asked Stevie.

"In a Puerto Rican neighborhood, outside of Newark. In a city in the state of New Jersey."

"Oh Christ," said Stevie.

"You got something against New Jersey?" Ferrer asked, faking that he was ready to defend the state from any bad-mouthing.

"No, no," Stevie said, "it's just that we hoped to see Soto soon." "He should be back in, let's see, four days, when the new semester starts," Ferrer said. "The day before I have to go back to Ohio," Sharon told Stevie. Another round of beers and a vodka on the rocks for the portrait painter.

They had two more days together, which they spent at the private beach behind the Caribe Hilton Hotel, sneaking onto it from the adjacent public beach by swimming around the jetty that supposedly separated the masses from the paying guests. They swung each other in hammocks between the palm trees, took dips in the pool and drank piña coladas from the beach bar. At Sharon's request, after dinner, whether at Burger King (once) or bringing store-bought meals to eat at Stevie's apartment, they spent their evenings walking around the Old City, going through the San Juan Gate which led them to the waterfront promenade bordered on one side by the bay and on the other the now massive-looking Spanish-built walls. They ran through blue cobbled alleyways and Sharon insisted on buying cans of cat food and a can opener from a colmado and opening the cans and setting them down on different streets where stray cats wandered. They kissed against buildings.

In the morning, Sharon packed and they called a cab and promised one another they would be in touch, and during the next school break he would go up to Ohio or she would come down to the island again or they would meet in New York, and Stevie carried her backpack down the stairs and the cab was waiting and they kissed and Sharon cried, and then she was gone.

Stevie went back to his apartment. He took his typewriter out to the balcony. Would he give Fico, the young cabin boy a short, sweet love affair on the island of Borneo? He meets the half-native girl and she shows him the interesting, and not so interesting, parts of the island, and they meet . . . pirates? . . . are held hostage, and escape? And then he has to leave on his ship, vowing to return to her one day.

Corny! Better, he stows away his love, a half-Dutch, half-Dayak native, aboard the ship, sees her every night in her hiding place. She is discovered by a member of the crew. The captain locks Stevie and the woman up until the next port. They go through the Suez Canal, then are thrown ashore in Egypt. Their adventures take them down the mighty Nile, around the sacred Pyramids, into the teeming Cairo streets.

TWENTY-THREE

I didn't notice it right away, but probably a couple of days after it began. It didn't seem that big a deal at first; but when I seen her face up close, that look like something kept her eyes glued on those spots, she couldn't pull them away no matter what, she was cleaning and scrubbing and then pushing so hard down with the Brillo and the other cleaning stuff, then I started to get a little, then a lot, worried.

She kept the house real nice, and the things I usually had thrown around, clothes and maybe some books and newspapers, they were all put away by the time I got home from the store. Nice. Coming home to a clean apartment. But then Carmen started with the scrubbing. It wasn't just stuff in the kitchen, all the pots and pans even when we didn't use them for dinner, but in the other rooms too, and even on the walls and the floor. Which made me tell her, "O.K., enough already," and she said O.K., no more, and then I'd come home again and she would be on her knees in the bathroom working like hell to clean out the ring around the bathtub and the ones in the sink and even in the toilet bowl.

I would come home and Carmen would be on her knees in the bathroom—who knew for how long?—scrubbing with steel wool and scraping with razor blades and cursing and even with tears in her eyes—looking up at me looking down at her, me angry, pleading, "I got to get this clean, Papi. If I don't get this clean, I can't do nothin' else."

I had to drag her away and sit her down in another room or on the balcony and give her a couple of glasses of brandy before she would calm down. Then we would eat and I would paint or write and she would go through the books I have about artists, looking at the paintings over and over, especially the Picassos and the Italian artist De Chirico, and any of the artists who would distort the way people really looked, or would paint scenes that looked like dreams.

"People could look like that up in your head and life could be creeping by, it don't have to be a dream," Carmen said of the paintings. "Sometimes I don't know where my eyes are because I ain't seeing what everyone else says they see, and people do things that could only mean something if it's happening in a dream, you know?"

I do and I don't know, but I don't answer when Carmen talks like that.

Then we would have our before-bed cognacs.

I woke in the middle of night to go to the bathroom, Carmen wasn't in bed. I went into the bathroom. She was down on her hands and knees, scrubbing that goddamn yellow stains around the bathtub and crying like a little baby. Her fingers were all cut and I had to bandage them up. Then I half-carried her into the bed and kept my arms around her and she kept crying, then –*gracias a Dios*—fell asleep.

The same thing happened the next night. She cut the cuts on her fingers and I bandaged them again. And she cried herself to sleep.

Then came the roaches and the rats. They started multiplying when the garbage men went on strike and garbage began to pile up all over the city. The electric company workers and the firemen threatened to join the strike. Power stations were sabotaged and some nights the lights went off. So things were starting to fall apart.

Then, for me, they collapsed, in a heap.

I should have known when I seen the kid. He was the same one that gave Carmen Manny's message in the plaza. The kid didn't look more than eleven or twelve, he was skinny with a little face like a small hungry animal. Except for his eyes, which were big and brown and liquid shiny like in a bad painting. I seen the eyes staring through the window of my store, and then they skittered away, and the kid followed. When I seen the kid, I felt something funny, but I didn't remember then who he was.

An hour later, the Italian fellow who runs the ice cream parlor came to the store. His face was gray, the same color as his short-cut hair. He told me I should go home, something happened. I asked him what happened. He looked all upset. "Go home," he said, "Rapid! Rapid!"

I started down Fortaleza Street. I felt sweat coming down my left side from under my arm. I felt my ass burning from my hemorrhoids. I felt my mouth completely dry. I felt a pain in my left side. A cat scooted in front of me, I almost tripped. I almost knocked into a hot dog cart on the corner, the guy behind it yelled something at me. I ran into the street to get around a mountain of garbage that wasn't picked up because of the strike and almost got hit by a bus coming into the plaza. It was like one of those bad dreams about running but never getting where you're trying to go.

There was a crowd on the sidewalk outside my house. I had to push my way into the hallway. It stunk from broken bags of garbage someone threw in there. There was a lot of people inside, including two cops. One of them was talking into a walkie talkie. The other was down on his haunches looking at something. I pushed through some more. I knew what I was gonna see. Carmen. Crumpled up again at the foot of the steps.

Her mouth was wide open. Her eyes were so puffy, you couldn't tell if they were open or closed. There was dried blood between her nostrils and mouth. There were large bruises on her cheeks. Her top lip looked five times its regular size. Tears were frozen on her cheeks.

I'm gonna be honest now and tell you what I felt seeing Carmen dead. There was the shock and tears and the fist punching at my heart; but also, I'm ashamed, there was relief. Like a burden was lifted. From both of us.

The cops asked me if I knew her and I said I did. They asked her name. They asked me more questions about her. I couldn't answer most of them. I told them she was staying with me and they seen the needle marks on her arms and gave me a funny look, but didn't say nothing.

We had to wait an hour down there in the hot smelly crowded hallway before some guy from the government came to officially say she was dead. Flies were landing on the bruises on Carmen's face and I went upstairs for a sheet and covered her with it. Finally, they took her away and I went upstairs again.

I sat in my old leather chair. I sat and I stared—at nothing. And I felt—nothing Then I was thinking of how the people I loved were taken away from me. And how I go on living. What I had to do to go on living. How I had to lie and cheat and steal. And sometimes worse, you want to know the truth. And every time I found out somebody I knew died or was killed, I had the same feeling I had when I seen Carmen. I was angry and relieved too because it was someone else, it wasn't me. And then the pain and the guilt and the crazy mad anger.

That's what it means to be a survivor.

Later that night I called Rosa, Carmen's aunt. She said she would leave Millie with a friend and come to San Juan in the morning and take care of the funeral arrangements. I forced myself to go to my workroom and do a painting. It had babies burning and pigs fucking in it. One of the pigs had a man's head. The head was pulled back and howling and there was dark sunglasses on the face which was pitted and scarred. After I finished the painting, I tore it up.

I sat up all night and at seven in the morning Rosa rang my bell. She was wearing the same red-checkered slacks and tennis shoes like when me and Carmen went to see her in the country. I gave her some coffee and then we went to the morgue. The coroner said Carmen died of a fractured skull from a fall. She also had a broken nose and a broken jaw, internal bleeding, two broken fingers on her right hand, contusions, lacerations, etc. Then we went to a funeral home, where they brought the body later in the day and I chipped in with Rosa a couple of hundred dollars each for a coffin she picked out, white with patterns on it. Rosa said she was going to bury Carmen in Barranquitas, where she was born.

The little cemetery was in the countryside, between green hills. There were statues of Christ and the Virgin Mary and different saints in niches over the graves. A lot of the graves were covered with wreaths of flowers, real and plastic. Even there in the mountains, where it was supposed to be cooler, the sun beat down hot and steady. It made me weak and dizzy.

Standing over the grave with me were Rosa and Millie and the priest—a guy with wavy brown hair and a horsey face—and Carmen's grandfather—a little twig of a man with a face like a withered tobacco leaf, he looked at least a hundred—and two of the guys who dress like girls from the all-night restaurant. The two of them were carrying on crying in their little black dresses and high-heeled shoes. Carmen's brother was there too. He looked almost like her twin. He had the same thin face, gypsy-dark eyes, and pouty lips. He wasn't much bigger than her either. He had a long scar on his left cheek that disappeared into his neck. He said he and the two girl-guys heard about Carmen's death "through the grapevine."

There was about a dozen people there from the barrio. They probably didn't know who was being buried, but it was something to do.

When they started shoveling dirt on Carmen's coffin one of the guys in a dress, he looked like the actress Veronica Lake with blonde hair falling over an eye, got hysterical and fell on the ground. The priest grabbed his legs and Carmen's brother, Rafi, took his arms and they had to carry him away. He fought real hard. The priest got kicked in the groin and he doubled over, still hanging on to one leg, and I had to grab the other leg. We took him back to the hearse and put him against the car's fender and he let out a blood-curdling scream like he was being put on top of a lit grill, it was probably almost that hot. We put him on the ground and he finally calmed down. I was soaked with sweat and felt like I was going to pass out.

After the burial, we went back to Rosa's house and onto the terrace. Millie and her grandfather sat on a wooden bench by the wall, holding hands. Neither of them said a word. They both looked dazed like something important might have happened, but they ain't sure what. The two guys in dresses were shooting down straight rums. Every once in a while a sob would escape from one of them and the other would break down. Carmen's brother was sitting quiet, drinking a beer. His face looked small and tight. Rosa and the priest were both drinking scotch. The priest kept talking about God's will and Rosa said if there was any justice, God would make sure the sonovabitch who beat Carmen to death was killed. Carmen's brother, Rafi, went to the edge of the terrace and looked out at the countryside below. After a couple of minutes, I went over to him.

"I gonna kill that cocksucker," Rafi said, he was talking to the scenery.

"Who you talking about?" I said.

"That motherfucker, Manny," Rafi said. "He came over looking for her. Said she owed him from drugs. I know he gave her some horse free, she shared it with me. That was before you brought her out of it again, she told me about it. That sonovabitch Manny he wanted to turn her on again. I told him to go fuck himself, she was with you and she was clean. He turned deep red and said she owed him and if she didn't pay he was gonna cripple her. I tol' him if he touched her I was gonna cut off his nuts. I know where to find him real quick. He got customers in the Condado he takes care of every night. I know, 'cause one of them's my cousin Pipo, he scores with Manny there in La Placita. I'm gonna go there and kill that cocksucker motherfucker."

I decided that I was gonna beat Rafi to it.

About fifteen minutes later, I left to go back to San Juan. When I got into a publico, the other passengers were talking about what was happening around the island. The electrical workers and the firemen joined the garbagemen in the strike. As we rode we heard over the radio that bombs were set off in power stations and in a couple of large American-owned stores and telephone lines were cut. All sorts of revolutionary groups were claiming credit. Then came a bulletin that a private guard was killed at an American-owned supermarket that was firebombed, and that the governor had called out the National Guard. All of which didn't mean nothing to me, I had other things on my mind.

When we got onto Highway Two there was a huge traffic jam leading into San Juan. By the time we crept into the city, it was dark. There were no lights along the streets for long stretches and the streets were almost empty of people. It was a spooky feeling, something tense in the air like some catastrophe was about to happen. We went along the ocean road leading into the Old City. All the lights along the road were out. The sky was gray with moving clouds and outlined against it like inky drawings were palm trees and church domes and spires.

The driver left me at Plaza Colón. There were lots of cops and soldiers in the plaza, which was lit up by searchlights on top of an army truck. The cops and soldiers were stopping cars and looking inside and directing the drivers away from San Francisco and Fortaleza Streets, both of which led to the governor's mansion. Behind the plaza, I didn't see no lights. It looked like all of Old San Juan was blacked out.

I went to my apartment and got a flashlight from the kitchen closet. Then I went into the bedroom closet and took out the attaché case. I put the case on the bed, opened it and picked up the gun. I put bullets into it. I went back outside, hoping I could find a taxi to take me to the Condado. Then I heard sirens and saw more army trucks and cop cars speeding through the plaza and into the old city. And when I turned I saw the sparks shooting in the air and the black smoke curling into the gray sky.

I went around the edge of the plaza and down behind the Tapia Theater and then to Calle Tetuan, which is just below Fortaleza Street. There was a cop with a white helmet on the corner. He moved around the corner and when his back was turned, I went down the street. It was dark and deserted, except for the people standing on balconies, all looking toward the orange sparks that were crackling and spitting into the sky and the white cinders that were falling like snow. I went two blocks down Tetuan, then turned up San Justo to Fortaleza. There were soldiers up and down the street, talking into walkie-talkies, and there were hoses all over the street. I could see more hoses being unwound from trucks on the next corner. Halfway up that street was the American-owned supermarket—and my store.

I ran down the block. Soldiers were manning the hoses and there was a truck aiming a light into the supermarket. Flames were leaping out of the front of the store. The water from the hoses gleamed like sparks as the stream was caught in the truck's light.

The fire had spread down the street, to the fabric store and the fancy Cuban jewelry store. And to my store too. The front windows of all the stores on the block were smashed and smoke spiraled out thick and black. Like the others, my store was going to be a total loss.

How did I feel, seeing all this? Seeing the end of my world? I felt . . . numb. I felt it was inevitable. I felt something repeating that had both everything and nothing to do with me.

I left my burning store without looking back at it and went to the Plaza Colón again, looking for a taxi. There wasn't any. I went down to the waterfront and began to walk to Condado. The lights were out down there too, but across the bay, in Cataño, lights flickered like low stars, and every now and then the real stars peeked through the moving clouds. A freighter silently slid by like a dark thought. I finally seen a taxi and hailed it. The taxi driver had the radio on and the announcer said a right-wing terrorist group just claimed credit for a bomb at the Socialist Party headquarters that killed a janitor there. The group said the bomb was in revenge for the ones set off at the supermarkets.

The lights were out on the Dos Hermanos Bridge and in the condominiums on the other side of the lagoon. The lagoon water, which usually reflected the lights like electric charges, was black. On the other side of the bridge, past the breakwater where one of the rocks was shaped like a dog's head, the ocean heaved like it was taking a deep breath.

We went down Ashford Avenue, which was crowded with cars. The street lamps were out, but light came from the hotels, which had their own power systems. Candles flickered from inside still-open liquor stores and tourist shops. Police and soldiers were out in front of the big tourist hotels. The cars had their headlights on and drivers were honking their horns.

I got out of the taxi and walked to La Placita, the little park behind Ashford Avenue, where Rafi said Manny did drug business. The park was surrounded by condominiums and expensive homes. During the day, West Indian maids took care of little kids who played in the park. In the mornings and evenings, people walked their poodles and German Shepherds. Tonight, the park was dark and deserted.

I stood across from the park under the canopy outside a Catholic Church that looked like a catering hall. The church was locked. I still had on the blue suit I wore at the funeral and the jacket partly covered the bulge of the gun in my pants pocket. The gun felt heavy against my sweaty thigh. I waited in the dark entrance. What was I thinking? Nothing much. I fought down thoughts of Carmen. I wanted only one picture in my mind: Manny, surprised as hell, big-eyed, bloody, crumbling from the bullet in his gut.

After about half an hour, a guy began circling the park. He was a young, thin fellow in a short-sleeve guayabera. He walked with jerky motions. He kept looking around and scratching his face. He went to the other end of the park, sat on the top of a bench with his feet on the seat. After a while, a car pulled up along the curb and he jumped down. It was the rusty blue Chevrolet with the pretzel fenders. Manny's car.

The guy went to the car, leaned his head inside the window, then stepped back as the front door swung open. He disappeared inside the car.

I walked real fast on the sidewalk between the park and the street. Just before I got to the car, the door opened again and the guy got out. He jerked past me, looking like a kid rushing off to a guilty pleasure.

The motor started up and I rushed the car and pulled open the front door which wasn't locked. Manny's head shot back and when he saw me leaning halfway into the car, his eyes popped. His features froze, then got small and tight like they were being screwed down into his face. He managed to push out a smile. He started talking a mile a minute.

"Mr. Wolf, my man! Hey, I been looking all over for you. That motherfucker Hector, he's gonna die for what he done to her. Listen, what happened is Carmen owed me some money, O.K.? Not that much, but one thing I learned, you got to collect your debts soon as you can, or people gonna take advantage of you. It's human nature, you know? So, Hector and me, we had it out about that night when you took me to the hospital—and don't think I don't appreciate what you done that night—Hector told me the other guy he was with fed him a ton of bullshit on how I did a double-cross on a deal, which I, personally, would never do when it comes to business, but Hector is one dumb motherfucker, he believed the guy for what actually was *him* ripping *me* off. So, Hector apologized and practically kissed my feet, 'cause he knows I never double-dealed him, or nobody, and the other dude played him for a fool. So, I told Hector all I wanted was for him to scare Carmen, you know? Just so she'll pay what she owes. So that fuckin' animal, he's such a dumb motherfucker, he didn't realize what he was doing and before he got his senses back, he . . . unh . . . you know, hurt her. Bad. And . . . unh . . . she got . . . unh . . . wasted."

Manny's mouth pursed up and his eyes glared at the steering wheel. "I'm gonna finish off that dumb motherfucker," he said.

"You ain't gonna be around to finish off nobody," I said and I pulled the gun out of my pocket. Did I believe what Manny said about Hector? What difference did it make? The thing was, Manny had to die. Not only for Carmen. For the others, for my wife, my daughter, all the others. For all kinds of things, going way back. To before Manny was born or I was born. Which made me just then crazy.

Manny saw the gun and his eyes ducked behind their slits.

"Fuck!" He leaned his back against the driver's door, pulled up his legs like he was trying to protect his chest. Then he kicked hard into my shoulders, and I tumbled back out the door and landed on my ass. The gun skidded away, against the curb, the pale glow of the moon shining on it. I crawled over and picked the gun up and stood and ran to the car. Just as it started to squeal away I managed to jump on the back fender then hold tight along the back. Manny seen me in the mirror and started swerving the car as we sped around the park. He turned the car toward Ashford

Avenue and skipped it up on the sidewalk there, blaring the horn, and people screamed and leaped out of the way. And I kept holding on, I don't know how. He bounced the car back into the street and slammed into a taxi. I half-fell, half-jumped off. Manny swiveled the car around and hit into a black sedan, then tore down a side street leading to the beach. The car crashed into a metal barrier at the end of the street.

I was up and running, feeling warm blood sliding down the side of my face. I saw Manny's legs as he got out of the car. I almost caught up to him, then slipped. I was down again; then he was over me. The sweat on his face, the whites of his eyes, his gritting teeth and the gun in his right hand all glinting. He pointed the gun at my groin. His chest was heaving real fast.

Then the black sedan came racing down the street with siren wailing. It screeched to a stop halfway down the block and four men came running out with guns in their hands, shouting, *"Policia!"* Manny took off over the railing and down the beach and I got up and followed. The moon lit a path on the black ocean in front of us. Manny got to the shore and ran along it. I was about twenty yards behind him. He got to the beach behind the Sheraton Hotel and all of a sudden two big searchlights flashed on from the terrace in back of the hotel. The policemen behind us began shouting and so did people from the terrace. Soldiers started running across the beach with rifles. They fell across the sand and pointed their rifles at us. Manny froze, then turned toward me. He was right in the spotlight, looking like his body was charged with electricity.

This was my chance. He was all lit up for me. A phosphorescent target. I stopped and held the gun with both hands. I aimed at his heart. My own heart was punching against my chest. I could barely make out his face, but saw his head jerk up and down like he was telling me to go ahead. To do what I had to do.

Then he raised his right arm like he was about to wave. A flame shot from his hand. He fired first. I shot my gun right after.

Shouts started coming from all over and rifles exploded. I felt a sting in my back. Manny twirled around like a ballet dancer and went down on his knees. Then he got up and staggered into the ocean like he saw something there he had to reach and was going to follow the moon's path to get to it. He dropped to one knee and a wave knocked him on his back.

Two soldiers came running toward him and lifted him under the arms and dragged him toward the beach. As they were pulling him back, I thought: Let that sonovabitch go. Let him go back into the sea, where he came from. Where he belongs. Back in the sea.

Then my legs turned to jelly and I was down on the sand and there was a rush in my head, it poured down through my body and pulled me under.

TWENTY-FOUR

Betty and Larry Cruz both looked perturbed. Betty even seemed a little angry.

"Why didn't you let us know what was going on?"

"So what would you have done?" Wolf asked from his bed at the Río Piedras Medical Center hospital. His left shoulder was covered with gauze and tape and a plastic tube ran into his left arm.

"We had to hear about Carmen, and about . . . the rest, from people in the street," Betty said. There were tears in her eyes.

"Everything happened so quick," Wolf said.

They told Wolf that when he was out of the hospital, he should stay with them in their extra room. Larry said he would look into what would happen with Wolf's store.

There was a faraway look in Wolf's eyes. He shook his head, then he nodded, then closed his eyes.

Doris Jackson was the next visitor. She told Wolf that after she saw what was left of the store, she went to his apartment, and when she didn't find him there, she went for a coffee at La Bombonera and heard the old regulars talking about a news report that said the owner of a jewelry store in the Old City was wounded by a gunshot on the beach behind the Sheraton Hotel. She bought a copy of the *San Juan Star* and in the last paragraph of the story about the strikes and fires, it said that the owner of a burned-out jewelry store in the Old City was wounded in a gunfight on the beach behind the Condado hotel and taken to the government hospital, and it couldn't be learned how or if the incident was related to the fire in his store.

What the hell was that all about? What happened?

"What happened, happened," was all that Wolf would say.

"Well, thank God you're O.K., and the strikes are over and everything is back to sort of normal," Doris said. Then she said: "Look, if you need anything . . . well, I'm here for you. Just let me know. I'll help in any way I can."

Wolf shut his eyes.

Doris took his hand, kissed it and left.

She waited half an hour for a bus back to the Old City. She wouldn't bring her new troubles to Paul (no job during the week, no paycheck yet from club owner Mimi for her weekend gigs, rent on her apartment due, John Jackson still . . . somewhere). Paul was her weekend guy, she didn't want to burden him, depend on him for the rest of the week, for the future. So Doris, you will have to find another Monday to Friday gig, keep the world, *your* world, spinning.

First, something to eat. A hamburger at Sam's Patio. Wash it down with . . . a goddamn Coke, rum-less and gin-less.

Stevie, the young guy from the store, sat at a table near the bar and waved to Doris when she entered. "Please," he said, "join me."

Doris smiled. *What the hell.* She sat on the chair he had pulled out across from his. He was drinking beer and munching on pretzel sticks.

"How about Mr. Wolf? Have you heard anything about him? Is he O.K.?"

Doris told Stevie she had just visited Wolf in the hospital, and he seemed all right. She didn't mention anything about a gunshot wound, but Stevie knew about it.

"It's all; over town," he said. "A gunfight on the beach in Condado. They said it had something to do with drugs. How could that be?"

"It was someone he was taking care of," Doris said. "An addict."

"Wow. Incredible!" said Stevie. "What the hell hasn't Wolf been through?" He gulped down his beer and ordered another. Doris asked for a medium rare burger and a Coca Cola.

"So now what?" Stevie; asked.

Doris shrugged. "And you," you still going to classes at the University?"

Stevie put his hand to his chin and nodded slowly, as though by mentioning it, Doris was making him consider whether he would continue. He chugged down his beer and poured the rest from the bottle into his glass. His eyes were going shiny.

"I'm ready to go to Borneo," he said. "You see, I met this girl down here and I guess I fell for her, hard, and she's gone, but I don't want that to mean she's not still with me, which means we'll be going to Borneo—I always wanted to see that place. So since she's half Dutch, half Dayak, meaning a native of Borneo, I'm going to go with her to help her look for her mother, who returned home to escape her husband, a real bastard who was always beating and berating the family."

Doris narrowed her eyes, then thought it was best to humor Stevie. "So when are you leaving?"

"We've already taken off," Stevie said. He pulled a black-cover notebook from under the short-sleeved white shirt hanging over his khaki pants. "We happen to be right in the middle of a cholera outbreak. So we're going to look for Sylvia's mom, who is a nurse, at the hospital that's located outside of Banjamarin. Anyway, here's what's happening." Stevie opened the notebook and read:

> Sylvia had these soft brown eyes. Her dark brown hair was pulled back into a ponytail. Her lips were full, very full. She had a nice, slightly curved jaw. Her skin was tanned. She didn't wear face makeup. Dangling from her ears were silver earrings . . .

"O.K.," Stevie said, turning a few pages, taking several beer slips, then reading again:

> We managed to hitchhike out to the hospital at the edge of the jungle. We arrived late at night and found a place to sleep in a longhouse, Which was built on high stilts near a river that disappeared into the forest . . .

The waiter brought the hamburger and Coke. Doris bit into the meat. A little too well-done.

> There were wicker baskets hanging from the ceiling. Believe it or not, in the baskets were completely decayed skulls from the Dayak's head-hunting days, which ended not all that long ago. The Dayaks had believed that taking a head would help their people, save a village from plague, bring rain, increase rice production and ward off evil spirits. I learned from Sylvia that Antoh, which are both good and bad spirits, were still at the center of life for some of the older Dayaks. Both the good and bad spirits could appear as an animal or a bird or in the shape of a gigantic human or even in trees and other objects. The masculine sun and the feminine moon were good Antoh. They were the parents of the stars. Like children everywhere, some stars were good, some bad . . .

"O.K.," Stevie said again. Our trip has just begun. You get the idea."

Doris nodded. *Keep at it, Stevie. You'll get there.*

Stevie drank more beer: "I feel terrible about what happened to Mr. Wolf," he said, "to the store, everything. I still got some books he lent me. We had lunch together a couple of times in the stock room, he sent out for sandwiches. He always wanted to know how I was doing, what I wanted to do with my life. I told him I wanted to write and that's when he piled the Conrad books on me. What the fuck can we do now, about him, it, everyfuckinthing?"

Doris shook her head. "I guess we just keep on going on." She added. "Good luck in Borneo."

"Yeah," said Stevie. "I guess we just got to keep looking for the good *Antoh* that pop ups, sometimes."

Later, in the evening, while sobering up as he sat out on his balcony, looking at the purple sky, Stevie chewed himself out.

Is this the way I'm going to confront tragedy, life, love—by just writing about it? What a dumbass!

He went to the phone and called the number Sharon had given him. He got her answering service. He left a message:

"It's Stevie, I love you and I miss you, Sharon. Say the word and I'm on a plane tomorrow and we'll meet and continue on to Paris or Madrid or a Greek island. I'm ready to go out into the world. With you. Or I'll wait until your semester ends. Just say the word."

TWENTY-FIVE

Every time the door opens the cold and damp rush in. Jesus just arrived, all bundled up in a green artic coat with a furry hood, pants tucked into galoshes. The coat is shiny with melting snowflakes. His round, thin-mustached, tropical face don't look at home inside that coat's furry hood. He goes behind the front desk, he's the night clerk, takes off his coat and throws it over a chair there. Then he sits at the switchboard. He's wearing a heavy wool turtleneck sweater, but he's still shivering. "I'm gettin' pneumonia," he says.

People coming into the lobby stamp their feet and knock the snow onto the threadbare green rug and leave wet footprints to the elevator.

I lean back on the brown plastic couch and light up a cigarette. I just started smoking again after giving it up a dozen years ago. I been depressed lately. A lot has to do with the weather. It's been cold and damp. I got used to seeing the sun every day, which ain't been out here in a long time. My shoulder hurts when it's damp. They took a bullet out of there.

Manny survived too, the sonovabitch.

It broke loose when I was in the hospital. I had some visitors—Betty and Larry and then Doris, and a little after Doris left I felt the blood drain out of me, then come pounding back into my head, I thought I was gonna go crazy. I vomited up the lunch and cried and punched the walls until my knuckles ripped open. They tied me down to the bed and shot drugs into me until I quieted down. A psychiatrist came to see me and I kept telling him not to bother me and after the second visit, he didn't come back. The sadness was so heavy for days, it left me like I was paralyzed. The police wanted to know what me and Manny were doing on the beach that night. I told them it was none of their business. They said they were going to charge me and Manny with attempted sabotage and Weapons Law violations. But they were smart enough to figure out that the only thing me and Manny were out to do was each other. They knew my store had been burnt to the ground and they must have thought my shooting at Manny had something to do with that. Anyway, they didn't bring no charges right away and a couple of days after I got out of the hospital, I left for New York. The only one I seen before going was Slatsky. We met at La Bombonera. He offered to lend me money to start up my business again until I was able to collect the fire insurance. I told him it was time for me to leave Puerto Rico. He didn't say nothing further and neither did I. We shook hands and gave each other *abrazos* and I left.

I didn't go looking for Manny. I didn't know where he was, or how bad he was wounded. At first, when I got out of the hospital, I wanted to get another chance at that sonovabitch. But then I decided, the hell with him. I decided to . . . survive.

The snowflakes are soft white crystals swirling in the wind and shining in the light of the street lamp. Suddenly I want to go out in the snow. I go to my room and put on my parka and boots. When I come back into the lobby, Jesús is sitting at the switchboard with red wool gloves on. "*Coño!*" he says, "It's even cold in here. I should be back on the beach in P.R."

I step outside. It seems warmer in the street than in the hotel lobby. I walk up to Broadway. When I turn the corner, I get the full blast of the wind. It ain't so warm now. Cars are moving slowly over the packed snow. Rain is starting to fall and the rain and the snow are silver gleams in the cars ' headlights. Not many people are out in the street. I decide it ain't such a good idea for me to be there either and I head for a luncheonette to get some tea.

Then I see her, standing in a doorway, trying to fix an umbrella that the wind turned inside out. She's wearing a tight pink skirt and white boots and a short red vinyl jacket and a cigarette is hanging from her real red lips. Her red hair is piled up and around her head and she's got big brown eyes with blue mascara. There's a line of freckles across the bridge of her thin, straight nose. She's middle-aged and almost pretty except for the hard, pinched look in her face.

"You need help?" I ask her. She smiles. She's got crooked teeth.

"I just got my hair done," she says. "And stupid me, I didn't bring no kerchief or nothin'. Just this lousy umbrella."

"Let me see it."

She hands the umbrella to me. I try turning it all ways, but it can't be fixed. "I'm sorry," I tell her.

"Forget it," she says.

Then I see something strange in her. The way she looks and the way she stands. The way her smile is quick and real. The way she seems vulnerable and hard. I see Carmen in her.

I see Carmen in her face. I mean the woman's face is still there, but so is Carmen's. And then I see Sarah in Carmen, and Rachel in Sarah. I bite my tongue, but I can't help it, I see them like Chinese boxes, one inside the other. I see them all dragged away and pushed under and my knees get weak and I stumble and put my hand against the store window.

"Hey, honey, you all right?" the woman asks.

"Yeah," I tell her.

"Fifty bucks down the drain for this damn permanent," she tells me. "Oh, well. I'll find a way to get it back." She smiles at me. It's a warm smile, from the heart. Then she takes off running down the street, tossing the umbrella into the trash can on the corner.

I have trouble breathing; it's like I forgot how. I gasp and cough. I cross to an island in the middle of Broadway and sit on the edge of a snow-covered bench there, gasping and coughing.

Sleet falls against my face and I can feel it freezing on my beard. Gusts of wind are blowing snow off the benches across from me and turning the snow into little swirling tornadoes. Gradually my breathing rhythm comes back.

Then a calm begins to settle inside me. It spreads to my arms and legs and into my head. Like I been drugged.

I get up from the bench and cross the street again. On my way to the luncheonette, I glance in the doorway where I saw the woman. Of course, she ain't there no more. Maybe she never was. Carmen and Sarah and Rachel weren't there, and I seen them too.

In the restaurant, I buy a container of tea to go. Then I buy a hot chocolate for Jesus which is his cold weather drink.

Back at the hotel, I give Jesus the hot chocolate and sit back on the couch.

"*Gracias, amigo,*" Jesús says. He takes off his gloves and starts drinking and gradually some color comes back into his flabby gray face.

"Hey, that's just what I needed," he says. "I feel a lot better now. Like I ain't dyin' from the cold no more, you know?"

I grunt and drink from my container. The hot tea feels good going down.

I'm thinking: too many are gone, while I keep going.

I keep coming through and coming back, but what about the others?

Too many of them, they're gone.

O.K., you get another chance to settle up. To shake off the mud and the slime. To try again to make the connection—for yourself, for them—to what's worthwhile in this life.

Survivors will always find reasons.

Maybe I'll go back to Puerto Rico. I actually had a life there. Maybe I'll make some phone calls tonight. To Slatsky. Find out how is his family, how's business. To Doris Jackson, a woman with deep feelings for others. (And, I hope, for me too.) And that young guy, Stevie, I could always help him with more books.

One thing I learned, even in my old age. You shouldn't give up on people. Even if there's just a little light in there, trying to get out. You got to try to help. You got to!

ABOUT THE AUTHOR

Robert Friedman, who has had six novels published, was a reporter, columnist and city editor at the *San Juan Star* in Puerto Rico for more than 20 years and was the newspaper's Washington correspondent until it folded in 2009. While in Puerto Rico, he was also special correspondent for the *New York Daily News*. In his fiction, he has explored the colorful and often struggling lives of island residents who try to cope, both personally and politically, with the highly ambivalent Puerto Rico-U.S. relationship. Born and bred in the Bronx, New York, he now lives in Silver Spring, Maryland, just outside of Washington, D.C.